DEAD AND BURIED

MELISSA CLEARY

BERKLEY PRIME CRIME, NEW YORK

DEAD AND BURIED

A Berkley Prime Crime Book / published by arrangement with
the author

PRINTING HISTORY
Berkley Prime Crime edition / December 1994

ISBN: 0-425-14547-6

Berkley Prime Crime Books are published by
The Berkley Publishing Group,
200 Madison Avenue, New York, NY 10016.
The name BERKLEY PRIME CRIME and the
BERKLEY PRIME CRIME design are trademarks
belonging to Berkley Publishing Corporation.

PRINTED IN THE UNITED STATES OF AMERICA

10 9 8 7 6 5 4 3 2

For D.

PROLOGUE

After almost eighteen months in jail, Merida Green was going home. She had been incarcerated in the first place for murdering her former lover, a college administrator, and was also thought to have killed a young girl who had known about the crime. Shortly after Merida Green had started serving her sentence, she had managed to get someone interested in her plight. It was Alice Blue, a housewife and mother much respected in her community.

That had been enough.

Alice Blue had decided that Merida was blameless in the deaths and had trumpeted the quiet, fiftyish, well-dressed feminist's cause to anyone who would listen. Since it was such an odd conclusion, many did listen.

Merida Green became a recipient of media attention. They were terribly sympathetic, pretending for a moment to care for something besides selling shoddy products to people silly enough to believe what they saw on TV.

The press gave Alice Blue a great deal of favorable exposure. To be fair, they also provided an opposing view. The Honorable William Curtis, known to his admirers as "Big Bill," a long-time public servant who had gone down in the last election over that dreadful business of the missing Firefighters Widow and Children's Fund, often argued the cause from the community's point of view.

Despite this valiant effort at balanced fairness, the viewers at home somehow came to believe that maybe Merida Green wasn't as guilty as she once seemed. This notion, hammered into the heads of gullible viewers, then drifted on an odious breeze into the nostrils of politicians up for re-election.

Vox populi had spoken, they lied. Merida Green must go free. But how could this be accomplished? She had been convicted without a shred of doubt or protest.

Then the "Free Merida Green" forces got lucky. Judge Fuchs up and died. The event was not unexpected; he was, after all, well over eighty and had hung on to his bench only because senior circuit judges were obligated to try no more than one case a quarter. But it was a propitious event, for it allowed a crack for the right person to insert a wedge and bring the whole legal edifice crashing down.

The right person turned out to be the Honorable Jane Bellamy, mayor of Palmer (Jewel of the Midwest), who previously had not given the conviction of Merida Green much thought. Indeed Mayor Bellamy, who was rather self-involved to maximize her chances for personal happiness, hadn't considered the woman's plight at all except to say, "What of it?"

However, the avalanche of support (according to polls supplied by the "Free Merida Green" movement) showed Jane Bellamy that the honorable thing to do—well, the popular thing to do, anyway—was to throw her support one hundred seventeen percent behind Merida Green and her courageous grope for freedom.

Thus came the now infamous Thanksgiving, "There but for the Grace of God Go I," speech. The moving words and the spectacle of the "Iron Butterfly," Jane Bellamy, (her theme song was the popular "Inna Gadda Da Vida"), breaking down and bursting into tears on the air was so powerful that politicians throughout the Midwest immediately put through calls to Wilt Conewaring, the mayor's wholesale makeup supplier, to see if they could get some of those great fake glycerol tears, too.

The speech was successful. The parole board, made up of very rich appointees who were frankly tired of having people come before them who didn't seem to be very good people at all—in prison or out—were charmed by Merida Green.

"A winner," one appointee had written on his pad.

"Where did you get those darling shoes?" another appointee had asked.

They were charmed by Ms. Green's Boston upbringing and were absolutely fascinated by the book she planned to write, which suggested that Alma Hitchcock had been responsible for her husband Alfred's ideas.

If it were in the power of the parole board to do so, at least one of its officers would have offered this poor, put-upon, unjustly convicted woman a ride home.

As it was, Merida Green was soon freed.

A round of parties followed the release ceremony. There were offers of employment, but oddly, not one opportunity to pen her autobiography.

Things were slow in the book trade.

And while Merida pretended to be pleased and overwhelmed by the wonderful, wonderful friends she had made, and all the wonderful, wonderful things that had happened to her, the plotting for another murder began.

CHAPTER 1

The lieutenant hit the heavy door with his shoulder. Instead of opening, the entire door-flat toppled over.

"Cut!" yelled Stanley Gray the director, a little annoyed. He didn't get up from his chair, however. He was far too rich and famous for that.

The lieutenant, actually a ruggedly handsome actor, a little gray at the temples with an adorable round dimple in his chin, rubbed his sore shoulder. "You know, things like this didn't happen in the old days, Stan."

Stan Gray, a sixtyish former actor with a large head, lantern jaw, and a pot belly, nodded sourly and turned to listen to a production assistant whisper disasters into his good ear.

The lieutenant couldn't be more right. Things like this weren't supposed to happen. *In fact*, the director ruefully thought to himself, *this gig was supposed to be a snap.*

Stan Gray was a filmmaker whose most successful films had been a series of romantic comedies in the seventies with the likes of Robert Redford, Sidney Poitier, Barbra Streisand, and Dustin Hoffman. Now they, like him, had become directors and were now taking work away from their old mentor.

So, not having much choice, Gray, a man who in his

5

private life favored sober gray suits and thick horn-rimmed glasses (he was resembling, he realized, more and more, his father the rabbi turned insurance salesman), had gotten his white and maroon director's suit out of the closet. Stan Gray, sad to say, had accepted an estimated two million dollars, which would go right into his retirement account, to make a quick TV movie.

As the script was good and the actors were being brought back to play roles they had played before, Gray had confidently expected that he would be able to knock off this project without turning a hair. However, things had gone wrong from the beginning. The show—even though it was an all-star TV reunion movie scheduled to be released as a feature in Europe—had been beneath Gray's usual cinematographer and crew. So the veteran director had been forced to use an unfamiliar TV crew.

The actors, competent veterans all, hadn't worked that much in the last few years. *CopLady*, the project they were here reviving, had been a hit for almost eight years in its original run. Since the residuals were more than enough to retire on, that's just what the old cast had done.

Now, dragged back from their ranches and much younger spouses, they had been surgically and aerobically refitted and slapped back into service. Properly made up and outfitted, the veteran actors still looked attractive enough, but the whole chemistry, the lightning quick give-and-take that had characterized the old series, was gone. Professionals in the best sense of the word, the actors were all gamely trying, but their moment had passed, and Gray, a once-great director and teacher who essentially had been coasting for the last twenty years, was no longer up to whipping them into shape.

Only too aware of all this was Jackie Walsh, a perky, lightly tanned, thirty-something film professor from the

Midwest. It was Jackie's script to which the cast and crew of *CopLady: Back with a Vengeance* were doing such little justice.

"Keep saying to yourself," Jackie felt the warm breath and rich voice of the project's guest villain, Ronald Dunn, in her ear, "It's only a movie."

"It's only a piece of junk," Jackie whispered back.

"That is no fault of yours," Dunn assured her, taking Jackie's hands and looking deep into her eyes. "The script you and your partner have written is a thing of terrible beauty."

"And you are doing a grand job of playing Mr. Gloriously Evil," Jackie responded in kind.

"I simply speak your words."

"Come now," Jackie protested. "You're terrific."

"It's terrific," Dunn continued with what seemed to be great sincerity, "to play a villain who isn't a carbon copy of all the other villains I've played. Heck, I'm just happy not to be playing a baddie named Roy or Steve."

"Vic!" Gray's voice was heard. "Where is Mr. Dunn? Are you here, Ron? We're ready for Vic's first entrance!"

"Ready when you are, C.B.!" Dunn called out. He then drew Jackie into a quick embrace, but didn't kiss her as it would smear his makeup. "So am I going to meet you back at the place?"

"Eventually," Jackie smiled, reddening slightly. It was still very exciting to be with Ronald Dunn.

"You're not going to hang around here?" Dunn asked, somewhat amazed.

"Oh, *Vic!*" Gray yelled again. "Your audience awaits, my king! You know Hagman's still got his tongue out to do this part!"

"Just coming, Stan!" Dunn lied loudly. "Having a conference with the writer here."

"Conference her on your own time, Dunn!" Gray yelled
crabbily. "We've got a movie to make."

Dunn gave Jackie a wide-eyed "What can I do?" look and
Jackie, taking her cue, pushed him toward the set.

"Go. I've got errands to run. I'll see you later."

"Wear a stocking cap so I'll know you," Dunn called
after her.

Jackie turned to see that wicked, crooked smile and
blushed again. There was a reason, she had discovered,
why some actors work forever. They were genuinely a lot
of fun to watch.

As Jackie walked back through the building to the south
parking lot where her Jeep was parked, she reflected on her
summer so far.

It had been very nice.

Although she missed Peter, her son, who was going to
an eleven-week hockey camp in Wisconsin, Jackie had
enjoyed the time she had spent readying *CopLady: Back
with a Vengeance*. The script had come together easily. She
and her writing partner, Celestine Barger, had managed to
cannabilize an old two-parter they had written, which had
never aired, into a first-draft script that had been optioned
by Deutsch/Triangle, a new major ministudio.

The producers assigned to the project, a nice young couple with experience in the legal and recording end of the
business, had suggested very little in the way of changes,
contenting themselves with drawing up airtight contracts
and finalizing details for the TV movie's sound track.

Stanley Gray cared so little about what he was shooting
that he had not so much as read the script before the first
day of shooting.

The actors, just grateful to be working again, had accepted what they had been given without demanding a single
change.

But, after such an auspicious start, things had rapidly gone downhill. When Celestine returned to Palmer, Jackie moved in with Ron. Then, although she was technically on call for rewrites, Jackie was actually asked to do very little in the next few weeks, except go to parties and say bright, witty things about the production to the legion of newspeople who now stalked every set (pathetically hoping for something they could write about or put on the hundreds of magazine TV shows that now dominated the airwaves).

Putting all this behind her, Jackie left the building, giving a wink to the elderly security guard who whistled whenever he saw her legs. Once outside, the slumming film instructor donned her aviator sunglasses and strolled out to the parking lot. Tossing her keys from hand to hand, Jackie scanned the lot, looking for her companion in amateur crime sleuthing.

"Jake!" she called out.

After a moment, a big tan and brown German shepherd bounded over to her with a thin piece of metal in his teeth.

"What is that?" Jackie asked. "Put it down, Jake. It may be some drug thing. This is gang territory. I don't want you getting doggy *AIDS* or something."

"That's a slim jim, that's what that is," said a voice from behind her.

Jackie turned to see a familiar face. "Is that anything like a Spicy Pete?"

Mark Freeman, the jolly young animation specialist who taught at the same university as Jackie, laughed aloud. "No. This little beauty's for breaking into cars. May I?"

Jake raised an eyebrow when he saw this stranger reaching toward his snout. He didn't much like that.

Mark drew his hand back quickly. Jake then turned and gently laid the hastily abandoned implement in Jackie's hand.

"Thank you, Jake. So what do you do with this thing?" Jackie asked Mark. "Smash it against the side window?"

"No . . ." Mark said somewhat disgustedly. At twenty-eight, he didn't have much patience with those who apparently weren't as intelligent as he. Mark took the slim, crowbar-shaped object and pointed to a spot at the end where there was a thin strand of wire running between two metal prongs. "You drop this down the space between the side door and the window, engage the lock with the wire, pull up, and the door's open."

Jackie "hmmm'd," and then commented, "I thought that most new cars were modified to guard against that kind of thing?"

"They are," Mark confirmed. "This must be some old crook. Some guy in his thirties," he continued, intentionally needling his co-worker.

"A wonder he can get around without a walker," Jackie cracked.

"That's what I say," Mark responded. "I can't believe you wrote all those TV cop show scripts and didn't learn what a slim jim was."

Jackie shrugged. "This is TV, Mark! What do they care about what happens in real life?"

"Well . . . you got me there."

"Besides," Jackie teased in a mock haughty manner. "We solved only sophisticated crimes on *CopLady*. We left punk crimes to animation. Which brings us to the obvious question—how's your project coming?"

Mark snorted and then grinned. "*Teen Skater* is speeding along like a new pair of rollerblades. At this rate I'll be done in a couple of days. What about you?"

Jackie opened her car the old-fashioned way—with a key. "I'm going home tomorrow or the next day. They don't need me here."

"Come on, Jackie," Mark urged. "You're on a roll. You're going to go home and teach film finger painting when you can write multimillion dollar dreck of the week?"

Jackie shrugged again. "This is a one-shot deal, Mark. It's not like I've been turning down offers. Besides, Celestine and I had a bargain. She stayed home and took care of business all summer. Now I go home and teach and she comes out here in the fall to hustle our proposed revival of *Triumphant Spirit*."

"I don't get it," Mark threw up his hands. "It's not like you have to worry about rent here. Not as long as you're shacking up with a movie star, that is."

Jackie gave Mark a wilting look, then patted his protuberant belly. "You know, as long as we're butting into each other's business, Mark, I think I should tell you, it'd be a good idea if you lost a few pounds. Twenty at least. As it stands now, you look like a seven-foot man who's been squashed down . . ."

"Okay! Okay!" Mark whimpered. "You win. Uncle! Uncle! Is Nadia still in there?"

"I think so," Jackie said. Nadia Pitts, Stanley Gray's production assistant, was a former student of Jackie's who had moved to Los Angeles after graduation. Nadia and Mark Freeman had started dating when both got jobs working in Hollywood. They had been an item ever since.

"This is a big break for her," Mark said proudly.

"I just wish it were better," Jackie said sadly.

Mark's ears picked up. Like most professionals in show business, he loved to hear about other people's production problems. "What's the matter? The stars acting up?"

Jackie shook her head. "No, they're fine. And Stanley, even though he obviously isn't that interested, is doing a competent job. I just think cops and robbers have run their course for a while."

"Really?" Mark was genuinely surprised by the remark. "In this increasingly lawless world, you don't think people still enjoy seeing cops coming down hard on bad guys?"

Jackie watched with amusement as Jake took the slim jim in his mouth and took it over to an older car parked nearby.

"I just think," she responded, "that people are sophisticated enough these days to know it doesn't happen that way in real life. Criminals are back on the street the moment they disappear from the headlines."

"You're referring to Merida Green, I take it," Mark guessed.

"Not specifically," Jackie replied.

Mark, watching with Jackie as Jake slipped the slim jim down into the doorjamb and started to work it up and down to slip the car's lock, responded, "She's out?"

"Like poop through a goose," Jackie replied.

The door lock popped open.

Mark commented, "Poop."

"Yup." Jackie sighed, walked over and re-locked the car, and came back with Jake at her side.

Mark took a few steps toward the studio, but then turned to ask, "What are *you* going to do?"

Jackie shrugged and tossed the slim jim in the back seat as a keepsake. "Live my life."

"What if she makes another attempt on you?" Mark asked in what he considered to be a scary dramatic voice. "You won't have good old Lieutenant McGowan to help you."

Jackie gave the chubby animation artist a look, then said, "Aren't those pants a little long, Mark? I know it's hard to get the right length when you're forced to shop in the bigger sizes . . ."

"I'm kidding, Jackie! Geez!" Mark protested.

"Well, then," Jackie conceded. "I'll answer your question. In all seriousness, I think that if someone were threatening my life—especially a paroled felon who the police don't like any more than I do—that someone would come out to protect me. If not Michael, then another patrolman. And if no policeman did come, Mark, I wouldn't care if I died—because I wouldn't want to live in a town where the police wouldn't come for such a silly reason."

At that moment Nadia Pitts appeared. "Hi, Mark. Oh, hi, Jackie."

Jackie smiled as Nadia rushed past Mark and gave her a big hug.

"Oh, Jackie," the former film student gushed. "It's so good to see you. Thank you so much for recommending me for this job. I can't believe it's been two weeks and this is the first time I've seen you. Ooh! You're so groovy!"

Mark, feeling distinctly left out, turned to Jake and stuck out his hand.

Jake turned away uninterested.

Mark was crushed. "You too, hunh? So much for man's best friend."

In the meantime, Jackie finally disengaged herself and regarded Nadia in a friendly manner. "Look at you."

Nadia smiled and panted like a happy dog.

"Blond yet."

"It's amazing," Nadia grinned. "I woke up one morning and suddenly my hair was yellow."

"That is amazing," Jackie smiled with her. "How about the tan? Is that natural?"

Nadia looked at Jackie over one shoulder and then peeled down one of her halter straps to show the skin was tanned below. "I am totally amber."

"Wow."

Mark put his hands in his pockets and pretended to whistle.

Jackie knew that Mark wanted attention, but decided to punish him a little longer. "Well, Nadia. How do you like your boss, Mr. Hollywood God?"

Nadia stuck out her tongue. "Like blah."

"Has he started hitting on you yet?"

"Puh-leaze." Nadia groaned, rolling her eyes. "It's bad enough I have to listen to him. I mean, he never has anything to say. Just stupid stuff. Isn't he like a good director, maybe? Maybe *not*."

Jackie gave a small laugh. "He's done some things that hold up. They just get bored. They want to retire, half of them, but the studios throw so much money at them they keep taking the work. Do you realize Stan Gray's making more money for this picture than Georgiana Bowman made in her entire career?"

Jackie referred to the Hollywood legend, filmdom's first female director, who, after a long retirement in a rest home outside of Palmer, had recently been talked into making a limited comeback.

"Stinko," Nadia replied.

"Does anyone like that song, 'You'll Never Walk Alone'?" Mark asked. "I . . . I really think it's great myself."

"You know," Nadia continued, absolutely oblivious to her boyfriend. "I would have been just as happy if Georgiana directed this."

"Well, so would I," Jackie said, pushing her long, dark curly hair back out of her eyes. "But she's in her nineties. It's amazing she can handle teaching a master class once every other week."

"I guess." Nadia held herself a moment to keep from shivering. "Boy, it's getting cold."

"S'posed to rain," Mark commented, not really expecting anyone to listen.

"Yeah?" Nadia turned to her boyfriend.

"Uh, yeah," Mark insisted, happy to be part of the conversation again. "Look at the sky."

Nadia squinted at the depressing, day-old-coffee-with-skim-milk-colored sky.

"Very gray," Jackie confirmed.

Nadia looked at Jackie, remembered again how glad she was to see her, and gave the trim film instructor another hug. "Ooph."

"Listen . . . Jackie. You wanna come over? We can do a barbecue or something."

"Well . . ."

"We don't have any food in the house, Nadia," Mark pointed out.

Nadia turned and gave Mark a look. "Doi! Like, I mean, it is possible to stop at a store."

"It's pretty silly to be shopping for barbecue food when it's going to rain," Mark insisted. He knew that arguing with his girlfriend was a big mistake, but Mark Freeman, creator of *Teen Skater: Crusader for All That's Right*, was not about to back down from a fight.

"We-will-bring-the-hibachi-in-the-house," Nadia replied through clenched, capped teeth.

"What-about-the-smoke?" Mark answered in kind. "We got white drapes."

Nadia wrinkled her nose in disgust and turned back to her only real friend, Jackie. "He's very possessive. Have you noticed that? If Mark had his way, we'd be home like two or three nights a week totally, like, alone with just, you know, ourselves. And each other."

"Sounds horrible," Jackie confirmed.

" 'Young Love,' " Mark resumed. "That was another tune I always enjoyed. Although it makes me a little sad now."

Nadia grabbed Jackie's arm. "I'll ride with *you*. Give you directions. We're up in Topanga. Nobody can find us without Mark or me sitting right next to them. Unless they're a goat. Mark, you follow us."

"Why?" the young animator immediately protested. "I know where we live."

Nadia turned around indignantly. "Why do you have to make everything so hard? You know, Mark, for a guy who's fifteen years older than me, you're very immature sometimes."

Leaving her boyfriend wishing he had a pair of cool skates and a crossbow with an extremely accurate sight like *Teen Skater*, Nadia got into Jackie's Jeep and commented at once. "Cool."

"So," Jackie smiled, as she watched Jake investigating the five earrings on Nadia's right ear. "Do you miss dear old Rodgers U.?"

Nadia made a face. "Not really . . ."

As the young director's assistant talked, Jake gently removed her earrings with his teeth, inspected each one carefully, then gently returned them to Nadia's much pierced lobe.

"First of all," Nadia went on unheedingly, "I live with Mark enough of the time that it's like I never left Palmer. Then we're back home six months a year and I go down and hang out with the old gang when Mark's doing an An-Lab."

"But?"

"Well, sorry to remind us, but one of the old gang's like real dead." Nadia sat back and put her small, pink-sneakered feet up on the dashboard.

Jackie didn't like that much, but put up with it in order to draw Nadia out on her old roommate. Danielle Sherman, another gifted student, had been murdered during Jackie's third year at the college. Jackie had attempted to solve the case but things hadn't worked out quite the way she hoped. "Nadia, did you know they let Merida Green out recently?"

"Yeah. Ick."

"Yeah. You know, although they'd never admit this . . ." Jackie cut off a yellow BMW, then looked nervously back to see if the driver was brandishing a firearm. "I think that one of the reasons they've let themselves be persuaded to let Merida out early is because her first victim was so odious."

"You mean Phil? Yeah, what a creep."

Jackie gave Nadia a look. She doubted seriously that Nadia had actually been on a first-name basis with the former Communications Department chairman during his lifetime. "Yeah," Jackie commented, "he sure was. But it seems like everyone has forgotten that she also killed Danielle."

"I didn't forget," Nadia said quietly, nuzzling Jake's snout and shivering slightly.

"I haven't either," Jackie replied. "And neither has David Surtees."

"Yeah," Nadia rubbed her thighs reflectively. She had dated the Rodgers University film and video editing instructor a couple of times before getting involved with Mark. Like most of Surtees's friends, she suspected he would never again be as happy as he had been with Danielle. "So what are you going to do, Jackie?"

First of all, Jackie thought to herself, *I'm going to get past this older woman driving so slowly that a spider is placidly spinning a web between the tailpipe and the bumper.*

"I'm wondering," Jackie then commented, as she moved on around, "whether we shouldn't try to get the Palmer police to re-open the Danielle Sherman investigation."

"Why?" Nadia asked negligently. "If we already know who did it?"

"Well, we know, but there hasn't been any prosecution," Jackie pointed out. "I'm sorry. Call me Ms. Vengeance . . ."

"How about *Ms. 45?*" Nadia cracked.

"Even better," Jackie smiled. "I'm serious, though. I think a trial was in order."

"They figured they already had her," Nadia shrugged.

"Then they figured wrong, didn't they?" Jackie moved around a slow-moving station wagon full of nuns with a personalized license plate, *"OH B QUIET."*

"Do you really think they're going to do this for you?" Nadia asked.

"I'm not concerned that they do it for me," Jackie answered slowly. "I want them to do it for Mr. and Mrs. Sherman. For David Surtees and for Danielle herself. Whatever flaws she had, whatever mistakes Danielle made, she didn't deserve to end up with a syringe of heroin plunged into her heart."

Jackie slid by an elderly couple driving a Pontiac with a muffler that sounded like someone was methodically beating on the roof of their vehicle with a crowbar.

"Well, good luck."

All of a sudden, they heard a beeping noise.

"Something's cooked," Nadia commented.

"Hopefully not my transmission," Jackie responded, swerving slightly to miss being sideswiped by a man with a big wicker steering wheel.

Nadia looked around the interior of the Jeep. "You don't have, like, a microwave oven in here, do you?"

"I didn't when I woke up this morning," Jackie responded.

Nadia waited for Jackie to take the Jeep through a particularly tricky cloverleaf.

"But then," Jackie continued, "sometimes I come out to the car and find little gifts have been left for me."

"Is this some kind of creepy supernatural story?"

"I don't think so," Jackie said, shaking off an inadvertent chill. "I've got this temporary boyfriend," she explained, "who likes to surprise me with things."

"Do you mean Ron?"

"That's what I call him."

"How is that working?"

"What?"

"Dating a movie star?"

"Okay. I like him. You know how this kind of thing is." Jackie reached down and took a swig from a squeeze bottle filled with Goodwillie water.

"Not yet."

Jackie laughed and gave Nadia a look. The young girl with the platinum Lulu haircut at once grasped its meaning and laughed aloud.

"I'm not saying I'm ready to dump Mark. I like Mark."

"Not even for Luke Perry?"

"Well, let's not get crazy." All of a sudden the beeper sounded again. "What is that?"

Jackie looked at her dashboard panel to see if anything was flashing. Nothing was.

"Beats me."

"You were telling me about the 'Duke of Cicero'," Nadia reminded.

"I . . ." Jackie was about to blow Nadia off, but then thought better of it. What the hell? Why not say what it was like aloud? Sometimes by explaining something to someone else, Jackie succeeded in explaining something to herself.

"Well, what can I tell you, Nadia? Ron has money and that's nice. I've never been poor exactly, but I've never hung out in a mansion either. What else? He's not, you know, as big as he was. So it's not like he's mobbed if we go out. We've been together this summer because we're doing this project together. In a couple of days I go back to Palmer. And then I don't know what happens. Maybe it keeps going a little less intensely. Maybe we both move on. Ron is not really ready to settle down, yet. And I'm not ready, really, to plunge into a heavy relationship."

"Like with your lieutenant friend?"

Jackie felt a spasm of sadness pass through her. She had dated Michael McGowan, a homicide detective on the Palmer police force, on and off for two years. It had ended rather abruptly as they had both found other people. "That kind of just happened. And obviously Michael wasn't ready to settle down either."

The beeper noise was heard again. Jackie looked to Nadia. "Are you sure that's not you?"

Nadia looked down at her belt purse, then exclaimed, "Oh, my God. That's right! My beeper!"

Jackie rolled her eyes.

"I just started carrying it for the show," the young girl explained lamely.

"It can't be Stan Gray," Jackie mused. "He's accepting a nostalgia award tonight. In fact, I think they've already wrapped on the set."

Nadia shook her head violently. "This could be about tomorrow. I'm sorry, Jackie. But it might be important."

"How close are we to your house?" Jackie asked, pressing the accelerator down a little harder.

"Not very."

"Okay," Jackie sighed. "What should we do? Get off this road and try to find a Denny's or something?"

Nadia gave a coaxing, guilty little smile. "Actually . . . Mark's got a phone in his car if we can signal him to pull over."

"We can do that," Jackie said at once.

Making sure that Mark was following, she pulled into one of the "Need Assistance" pits off the Cal State.

As Mark pulled in behind Jackie's Jeep, he noticed nervously that the cars had tripped the big red "Need Assistance" light.

"What's wrong?" he asked at once, powering down the side window of his car.

Nadia reached in and unlocked the door. "Gotta use the phone."

Mark laughed. "For what? To win free tickets from Radio Frye and the Hairman?"

"Doi!" Nadia answered, putting on her seatbelt out of force of habit. "How about I got a page instead?"

"Oh. Excuuuse me!"

Nadia started to push-button the number on her red screen, then gave Mark a look. "Do you mind? It might be personal."

Mark got out of the car that the studio leased for him, taking great care to slam the door, walked up to Jackie's Jeep, and leaned his head into the window. "Sorry about all this."

"No problem," Jackie replied, tapping her driver's glove on the steering wheel. "I know it's not like this is your idea."

"No, indeed," Mark responded through clenched teeth. He then made a flabby little fist and asked, "You ever feel like . . . killing someone you really love?"

"Well, I do have a teenage son," Jackie replied. She reached into the pocket of her tan Banana Republic "millions of pockets" vest and pulled out a small package of

Spicy Pete Bites O' Beef. Opening the package with her strong fingers, she held it out to Mark. "Want one?"

"You know it."

Jackie then turned and poured the rest out on the carpet between the seats. Jake fell on his treat like the big dog that he was. "Listen, Mark."

"Yes, Ma'am?"

Jackie was diverted for a second by the music coming from Mark's powerful car stereo behind her. "What is that?"

"Power House. Anyway. . . . ?"

"Anyway," Jackie continued. "Nadia and I were talking about seeing if we can get the Palmer police interested in re-opening the Danielle Sherman investigation. Once we get back to Palmer, of course."

"Now see here," Mark raged, throwing his cheap sunglasses to the ground. "That's just the kind of harebrained, impractical notion she's always coming up with and . . ."

"That was my idea, Mark," Jackie pointed out quietly.

"Oh. Sorry." Mark reached down and picked up his sunglasses. One lens was cracked. The other was just dirty.

"Are you interested?"

"Uh, yeah. But isn't that kind of a political bombshell?"

This took Jackie aback. "What? Because Mayor Bellamy was behind letting Merida Green out of prison?"

"No, not so much that as Danielle's parents."

"I don't know them. Who are they?"

"Jackie, of course you know them."

Jackie could tell that Mark was still irritated with his lover. He wasn't usually so impatient with her. "Honest, Mark. I mean I may have met them somewhere. I say hello to a lot of parents at graduation and Founder's Day, but I can't for the life of me remember the Shermans."

Mark clicked his tongue with disgust. "Well, maybe

that's because their name isn't Sherman. Honestly, Jackie. Didn't you know that Danielle used 'Sherman' as her professional name?"

"No, obviously. Who are her parents then?"

"Curtis," Mark answered. "The ex-mayor and his ex-wife."

Jackie's heart dropped into her stomach. Big Bill Curtis, Palmer's former machine-politics mayor (who barely escaped indictment when it was discovered that he was tied into the organized-crime forces who had been responsible for, among many other things, killing an undercover cop, a Palmer hero and Jake's former owner, Matt Dugan) didn't really matter to her. However, the former Mrs. Curtis, Jackie was only too well aware, was affianced to Jackie's ex-husband. "Oh, boy," she breathed.

"It gets worse," Mark continued.

"I can't see how."

Jackie looked up and saw how. A Los Angeles Highway Patrol vehicle had just pulled in. The dark-haired film instructor wasn't all that familiar with Los Angeles driving laws, but she more than suspected that pulling into a motorist emergency area was illegal unless you actually had an emergency.

Mark Freeman, expecting a beating, immediately covered his head with his arms.

The solo LAPD officer got out of the car and walked over as slowly as a gunfighter in a Clint Eastwood Western. On the policeman's left hip resided a holstered gun the size of Jackie's forearm. In his right hand the cop held a ticket book that weighed far less, for it was nearly empty.

This highway patrolman _loved_ to write summonses.

Fortunately for Jackie, however, Jake's bark tipped her off that this was the one patrolman in all of California who she didn't have to worry about. It was Sergeant Hippolito (don't call him Hippo) Lavan, an old friend who recognized both Jackie and Jake.

"You! What the hell are you doing here?"

Jackie smiled widely and took off her sunglasses so the policeman would be sure to know it was her. "I figured if I pulled over and waited long enough, you'd eventually happen by."

"Terrific! How the hell are you?"

Jackie opened the driver's side door and got out. She then gave Lavan a quick embrace. "I'm fine. And you?"

"Super. What brings you to Smog City?"

"Work," Jackie smiled. "I actually like Los Angeles in the summer. I don't know why."

Lavan took the opportunity to mop his brow with a big red bandana. "Don't ask me either. What kind of work? Teaching? Sleuthing?"

"Writing," Jackie answered. "I still do teleplays when they let me. My partner and I just sold a *CopLady* reunion film, to ITV."

"*CopLady*?" Lavan's smile muscles rippled. "With Hal Ehrlichman? He's my hero. The man who got me interested in being a cop. Damn tough hombre for an Anglo. He in it?"

"Yes," Jackie nodded, "the whole gang's back. Hal doesn't knock down doors the way he used to, but he still looks great. Margot Diedrickson still has those great legs, Bronk Zarrakan still chews a toothpick and talks out of the side of his mouth, and Ronald Dunn is still as impossibly suave as the guest villain."

"Whoa! You better watch yourself with that guy."

"Too late," Jackie grinned. "I've already fallen into his clutches. In fact, I'm spending the summer out at his place in Redondo."

"Well, great," Lavan replied, obviously a little jealous. "You look good."

"So do you, thanks." Jackie gave Lavan's patrolman uniform a once-over. "So you're back on the Easy Rider highway, I see. I hope you didn't get into any trouble over . . ."

Lavan gave his booming laugh. "No, no. Not at all. Actually, I requested this. I was getting pretty bored hanging around the station. I didn't pump iron for seventeen years so I could type reports with two fingers. And that's all I was going to do with Straussey out of action."

"Oh, no," Jackie exclaimed, recalling Lavan's beautiful, bitch elephant mastiff who, along with Jake, helped corral a dangerous Palmer murderer before he could poison the town's water supply. "What happened to her?"

Lavan motioned with his head. "Your friend Jake there got her pregnant. Look at him. You big guilty so and so."

Jake didn't look all that guilty, but Jackie laughed anyway. "That's great!" she responded.

"You say so," Lavan replied dubiously.

Just then Nadia interrupted the conversation with a yell. "Jackie!"

"Excuse me," Jackie asked before rushing over to the passenger side of Mark's car.

Nadia was waiting for her, holding the phone out the window. "Unbelievable, right? I call two different numbers, they both kept me on hold so long I thought I was going to need to get a haircut and it turns out to be for *vous*."

"Sorry." Jackie, a little surprised, took the receiver and said, "Hello?"

Much to Jackie's surprise, the dulcet tones of her department chairman, the distinguished, former epic motion picture director, Ivor Quest, came through the cheap phone. "Jacqueline. Ms. Walsh. Are you there?"

"Yes," Jackie admitted, puzzled. "What's wrong?"

"Well . . . you're right in thinking something's wrong, Jackie. . . ."

Waves of panic swept through Jackie as she pictured one disaster after another. Had something happened to her son? Her mother? Had her duplex burned down? Had her last college physical disclosed some hidden malady? What could it be?

Quest continued, "I'm afraid there's been another death here at the college, Jackie. Another killing, in fact. And the university was hoping you could lend your well-honed skills to the investigation."

Jackie's reaction wasn't relief. It was instead, anger. "You called me out *here*, Ivor? To help investigate a murder that happened when I wasn't even in Palmer? I am not a private detective, Chairman Quest! I am a film instructor. If you need someone to investigate for the university besides the regular police department, why don't you get your head of security to do it?"

"Yes," Quest answered slowly. "You mean Mr. Hopfelt? Well, that's the thing. He can't, you see."

"Why not?"

"I'm afraid, Ms. Walsh, it was Walter Hopfelt who was murdered."

CHAPTER 2

The drive back to Palmer was no easy matter. Having her Jeep and Jake with her—since she hadn't wanted to crate him up on an airplane—Jackie was pretty well obliged to drive. When Mark and Nadia offered to pay all the expenses in exchange for hitching a ride (since they'd had to leave the studio-leased vehicle behind), Jackie couldn't very well refuse. For one thing, she still hadn't received her check from the *CopLady* production office.

Unfortunately, the young couple, nice as they were, caused nothing but problems.

They had delayed the trip by stopping at the Nita Naldi Pampering Parlor where Nadia tried, without success, to cash in a foot-sanding coupon. Then, the second day out of Los Angeles, the three travelers had spent most of the afternoon in a Pecos, Nevada, emergency room when Mark felt something sharp in his throat after biting into a Road Side Rest club sandwich. It turned out that he had swallowed a tack.

Finally, after listening to the couple fight for the final three hours of the drive about whose digital watch was more accurate (Mark's was more expensive but Nadia's accounted for the yearly leap second), Jackie dropped off her passengers at Mark's Cuthbert Street apartment and proceeded to Armstrong Hall, where Ivor Quest, Algernon Foreman, the acting president of Rodgers University, and

Dean Provost Ashley Landis were waiting for her.

This gathering constituted a fairly impressive group by Palmer standards, but the film instructor was too road-weary to go home and change. So tired was Jackie, in fact, that she didn't remember, until she got to the top of the stairs and crossed the threshold of the president's outer office, who the new president's administrative secretary happened to be.

The eyes of Polly Merton positively lit up as she saw Jackie approach. It was the work of a moment for her to push down the button of one of the president's two direct office lines and call herself on the other. Then, as the phone rang, Polly held up her hand to Jackie as if to say, "wait a minute," while she pretended to answer the phone. "Hello, university president's office, this is Miss Merton."

Jackie, unaware of Polly Merton's contrivance, regarded the secretary with a mixture of fear and loathing. For two years she had put up with this infuriating, apparently ageless, virago. The gargoyle of the Communications Department, Ms. Merton had taken advantage of the inattentive former communications chairman, Philip Barger, to set herself up as the queen of an impossibly complicated bureaucratic system.

When Ivor Quest officially succeeded Merida Green as department chairman, he had managed to get the far-from-pleasant Polly moved over to the English Department. There, the prim and proper Ms. Merton (whose taste in dress tended to run toward severe, almost nun-like, black or white outfits), had terrorized that department until Dean Foreman, taking advantage of his appointment as acting president, had succeeded in moving the secretary again, this time over to the president's office. It had been hoped that here Ms. Merton would be out of the way.

No such luck.

Finally, Ms. Merton condescended to put herself on hold. Then, picking up a lethally sharpened pencil and poising it over a memo pad marked "From the Office of the President," she asked Jackie, "May I help you?"

"Hello, Polly," Jackie forced herself to say in a cheerful manner. "I believe President Foreman's waiting for me."

Ms. Merton's countenance changed to one of studied bafflement. "Are you referring to Acting President Algernon Foreman?"

Jackie gave Polly an, "Oh, you kid!" look and then replied, demurely. "Yes."

"Just a mo-ment, please." Ms. Merton deactivated her hold button and again pretended to speak to another party on the phone. "Hello? Yes, sorry to delay you. There was a disturbance."

Jackie bristled. All summer she had dealt with secretaries who were almost excessively polite and helpful. They may have been out-of-work, would-be film stars, sniffling from drug use, blotched and leathery from cut-rate plastic surgery and too many years of being perfectly tanned. They even may have been utterly unable to type, file, or take dictation, but each and every one of those young ladies had been most proficient at acting the part of a friendly courteous secretary.

"Yes," Polly continued, raising her voice so as to intentionally invade Jackie's daydream, "you were waiting to talk to President Foreman. I'm sorry, sir. No, I'm afraid he's busy. No, I'm sure he isn't preoccupied with anything *really* important, but he did leave orders not to disturb him. Yes, I'll take your message. Just a moment."

Ms. Merton touched the "hold" again and flashed Jackie a cold, malevolent smile. "I'm so sorry. I'll buzz *Acting* President Foreman in a moment. *Unfortunately* I can't use the intercom when somebody's on hold. I've asked them for a more efficient telephone arrangement, but no one ever pays the slightest bit of attention to the requests of a humble secretary." Ms. Merton then disengaged the "hold" and told her imaginary caller, "Sorry, sir. What? No, leave as long a message as you like. I have plenty of paper."

Jackie was looking around for something to brain her with when the president's door opened and Ivor Quest called out to her.

"Jacqueline! You are here. I thought I heard your voice. Goodness. Have you been waiting long?"

"A few minutes," Jackie replied evenly.

"For shame, Ms. Merton!" Ivor said at once, grabbing the back of Polly's swiveling desk chair and giving the secretary a good spin. "President Foreman!" Quest then called out, "your dragon of the gate has kept Ms. Walsh cooling her heels in your anteroom."

Ms. Merton, although dizzy, abandoned all pretense of speaking on the phone and answered in her archest tone. "Perhaps you've forgotten, Chairman Quest, that I no longer work for Communications and you have no right whatever to comment on my efficiency."

"Nonsense," the handsome, silver-haired Quest responded. "Even though you are blessedly far away from us, Ms. Merton, I assure you that the entire Communications Department still holds you in the very lowest of esteem and furthermore . . ." Quest snatched the pencil out of Ms. Merton's hand and broke it in two. "I shall always consider it not just a pleasure but a responsibility to tell you what a useless impediment you continue to be!"

Jackie applauded briefly and then stopped to pick up her shoulder bag. Quest went back inside and Polly took the opportunity to get in one last jab. She looked Jackie's outfit up and down then commented acidly, "Isn't that by that Japanese designer? Funny, I heard they didn't need ironing."

Jackie, embarrassed that she hadn't changed out of the clothes she had been driving in, entered the president's office without commenting.

As she came in, Jackie heard the disheveled dumpling, Acting President Foreman, moan in a voice very much like that of the cartoon character Droopy Dog, "Isn't it unfortunate that, with all the killers and killings we've had in our little university, that woman out there goes on and on? In this age of witless plea bargaining, why couldn't we have let one of our murderers off with a slap on the wrist in exchange for plunging a ski pole into . . . ?"

"President Foreman!" Jackie exclaimed, genuinely shocked.

"I really think not," Ivor Quest, garbed like a Jamaican plantation owner, responded.

"Sorry, sorry," Foreman muttered, holding up his hands in supplication. "I am depressed. *One*, because of that woman who continues to be my secretary; *two*, because the Search Committee has turned up no candidates as yet to replace me as president . . ."

"We are trying, Algernon," replied Ashley Landis, the exquisite dean provost and chairwoman of the University Board.

"No, it is Ms. Merton who is trying," Quest quipped.

"*Three*," Foreman continued, as if the others hadn't spoken. "Because the university is embroiled in another homicide and *four*, as a consequence of my trio of depressions, I have taken to drinking heavily in the afternoons."

"There, there, Algie," Quest soothed.

Ashley Landis rolled a piece of paper out of the typewriter she was sitting at and turned to give it to the beleaguered president. "Sign this."

Foreman moved his bourbon highball aside and looked blearily at the printed form in front of him. "What is it? If it's my soul you want, I forfeited that when I entered academia."

"It's a transfer order, Algernon," Ashley replied.

"Where am I being transferred to?" Foreman pouted. "I don't know anything but English literature, and damn little of that."

Ashley shook her head impatiently. "Not your transfer, Algernon. Hers."

Foreman looked at Jackie in surprise. "Ms. Walsh's?"

"Ms. Merton's!" Ashley exclaimed.

"Oh, her. Good!" Foreman started to reach into his breast pocket for his Mark Cross pen and then stopped himself. "Can I do that?"

Ashley nodded. "You are the president."

The realization slowly swept over Foreman. "By God, it's good to be king!" Then, brandishing his pen like the mighty Conan would a broadsword, Algie Foreman applied his signature with a flourish. "Go, woman—and darken my door no more!"

He then turned to the others. "Can one of you slip this under her blotter on the way out?" Ashley Landis pocketed the note.

Quest turned to Jackie. "Ms. Walsh. Thank you for coming. Dean, shall we get down to the matter at hand? I think we've wasted enough of Jackie's time. Welcome back, incidentally." Quest favored Jackie with a ten-thousand-dollar smile. His dentist had been the richest man in Hollywood. "Your new amber color is set off wonderfully by that remarkable outfit. Miyagi, isn't it?"

Jackie nodded, as always tickled pink by her chairman's compliments and his warm, fatherly attitude. "Yes . . . thank you."

"It is we who thank you, Ms. Walsh," Quest said, giving her an elegant bow, "for cutting your vacation short to assist us here."

"The least she could do," the suddenly querulous Foreman remarked. "She being an administrative vice president and all."

"Really, Algernon," Ashley protested, anticipating a Jackie explosion. "You gave this poor woman a title with no real authority and expect her to work miracles with it?"

Foreman, now positively reveling in the power he wielded, waved his hands. "She wants authority, give her authority. Write something out. I'll sign it. I'm a signing fool today!"

Quest chuckled and attempted to get things back on track. "Indeed you are, Algie. Perhaps, Ashley, you—or Ms. Merton's eventual replacement—can draft something that will give Ms. Walsh the authority, at least in the university's eyes, to conduct investigations. Now, Jackie. Let us tiptoe out before President Foreman succumbs to the demon alcohol . . ."

"You know," the ever-suggestible Foreman responded, putting his hand on his stomach, "I am feeling rather bilious."

Quest continued, " . . . and investigate the *locus en quo* as Dean Westfall would say." Seeing the questioning looks of Landis and Foreman, the former motion picture titan explained, "I mean, of course, the scene of the crime."

As Ashley Landis broke the bad news to Polly Merton, Jackie and Ivor Quest left through the side door of President Foreman's office and walked down the narrow corridor toward the back of the building.

On the walls of the seldom-used back corridor there reposed a wealth of paintings, drawings, and etchings that had formerly hung at other sites on campus, but had been quietly removed over the years to this back corridor as their subject matter was found by incoming generations of students to be politically incorrect.

A minor Frederick Turner hung on one wall. It had been deaccessioned when the scholars had decided that his sunsets were not actually depictions of nature but instead rather lewd views of his favorite models.

A Wyeth "Helga" right next to it had been banished for similar reasons. Why contribute to the "Myth of the Mistress in Art" scenario, which had been so thoroughly debunked by Rodgers professor emeritus, Emma Artemis Brown?

As Jackie and Quest pressed on they passed a Lafcadio Hearn print that had been hidden so as not to awaken the issue of internment in the minds of the university's seven Japanese-American students, and finally, sadly, they swept past striking photos of African-Americans, taken by one of the university's most generous benefactors, the late great photographer, Sabin Hughes. These thrilling photo blow-ups had been tucked away until the thorny problem of slave reparations had been at last settled in the higher appeal courts.

At the end of the gallery, Jackie and the department chairman emerged from the corridor into an old high-ceilinged hall lit by a chandelier's one remaining bulb.

As Ivor Quest hunted through a giant ring for the right key, Jackie commented, "This is all very . . ."

"RKO Hitchcock, I know." Quest gestured off-handedly to the walls around them. "This is Sabin Hughes's old place. The entire building, I mean. These backstairs were for the servants. Being black, he was embarrassed by the fact that he had Negro servants, so he hid them."

"I see," Jackie lied.

"Up there . . ."—Quest pointed up the vertiginous *Psycho* stairs to the two landings above—"were the servants' quarters. Gorgeously appointed, or so they say. When the great man gave his residence to the university for tax relief, it cleared out all the furnishings the servants hadn't taken with them over the years and gave them to the theater department."

"What's up there now?" Jackie asked, as Quest finally opened the locked closet in the hallway.

"Nothing much. Storage. Fan-fold computer paper. Extra stationery of deposed administrators. Bathroom supplies. Did you ever notice that? Whenever someone has a huge house there will always be a guest bedroom just stuffed with toilet paper." Quest handed Jackie a flashlight. "Take this and follow me. First we go up, then we go down to the basement."

"Why do we need the torches?" Jackie asked.

"Torches. Ah, yes. A word from my youth." Quest flicked on his flashlight and led Jackie to the stairs. "Watch your step. The treads are mushy and the molding crumbles at a touch."

Following the older director and trying to step in the same places he did, Jackie asked, "Was he killed up here?"

Quest ruminated a moment. "Well, that's hard to say. I mean, how do we define it when a man receives the precipitating blow in one spot but actually dies in another? Let us say we are visiting first the place where Walter Hopfelt started his journey toward death."

Quest used his flashlight to indicate a break in the railing. "That's where Mr. Hopfelt went over. Careful. Now look here." Quest shined his light on a peg near the baseboard.

Jackie knelt down to inspect it closer. "What is it?"

"Just a peg. But three nights ago it had a tough piece of nylon line tied onto it, running from here to . . . there."

Jackie followed the beam of the light until it shone on a hardware store button hook screwed into the base molding several feet beyond the doorway immediately to the left.

"So Walter Hopfelt tripped over the cord and fell through the railing?"

"Yes, exactly." Quest offered Jackie a hand and helped her up.

"They took quite a chance . . ."

" . . . That he would fall just the right way?" Quest interjected, impatiently completing Jackie's sentence. "Yes, that was my comment. Then the police showed me this . . ." The communications chairman led Jackie into the room. He turned on the light, then winced as Jackie let loose with an involuntary shriek.

"Sorry," she said.

"Quite all right," Quest smiled thinly. "When I first saw it I screamed like Elsa Lanchester."

"What is it?"

"Let's get closer, shall we?"

Glad to have anyone, even Ivor Quest, beside her, Jackie moved closer to the thing in the chair.

"It's some kind of dummy," Jackie said. For some reason she found herself speaking in hushed tones.

"Yes." Quest tapped his left hand against the painted head. The dummy was made to resemble a teenaged girl with long brown hair. "Probably from the Theater Department—or Ashley Landis suggested it may be a clothes-building figure from Life Skills."

Jackie tentatively touched the pale figure's face. Her eyes then traveled down and all of a sudden Jackie recognized the jacket. "Oh my God!" she cried out.

Quest shuddered and held his heart so it wouldn't attack him. "Oh, dear. That one I wasn't ready for."

"I'm sorry," Jackie said, immediately solicitous. "Are you all right?"

"Yes, yes. I shall later consume all the liquor President Foreman manages to leave, but it's all my fault, of course. I should have explained to you quite thoroughly, as Provost Landis suggested, instead of playing it as if it were a dramatic scene in a thriller and I was still a bloody film director." Quest mopped his brow with a silk handkerchief, then seemed to regain control of himself. "I'm sorry. Anyway, you were screaming some revelation."

"Yes, indeed." Jackie excitedly pinched the mock satin material of the dummy's jacket. "Do you know who this belongs to?"

Quest looked at the large purple Rodgers U. "The Excellent U" jacket and shrugged his shoulders. "One of the students, presumably."

Jackie held up the flap of the jacket with a name on it. "Yes. This jacket belonged to Danielle Sherman."

"Great Caesar's ghost," Ivor Quest exclaimed. "The one who got murdered! I never met her, of course, but oh dear, indeed . . ." Quest sunk to the edge of the wooden L-shaped desk the dummy was seated in front of. "I . . . I . . ."

"Are you . . . ?"

Quest waved the question about his health away. "Are you quite sure?"

Jackie nodded.

"Then what are we talking about here, exactly?" Quest choked out. "Don't hold back. I've read those Teddy London stories. What are we facing? Ghosts? Vampires? Something . . . gelatinous?"

Jackie's bewilderment won out over her urge to laugh. "All this means, Ivor, is that someone got ahold of Danielle's jacket. Maybe even in a thrift shop. One presumes her parents donated her clothes after she died."

"Goodness. How ghastly." Quest shook his head with distaste. "So was Hopfelt supposed to recognize this girl and think she was a ghost?"

"Perhaps," Jackie said, drawing into herself to think this through.

Quest loosened the knot of his ascot. "Well, then. It makes it far more likely that this was a malicious murder and not just a prank. Look at the head, near where the ear would be."

Jackie explored the jawline of the dummy and uncovered another button hook. She felt the piece of nylon thread and followed its path over to an area behind the room's heavy door. "So someone tugged on the string when Hopfelt turned on the light."

Quest nodded. "That would be the assumption, yes."

The horrible thought flashed through Jackie's mind an instant before she said it. "And whoever pulled the string probably said something to him."

"I'm ba . . . ack!" said a female voice.

Jackie and Ivor both jumped.

Ashley Landis stuck her head into the room. "What are you two up to? I thought this would take ten minutes."

"Ashley, dear," Quest choked out. "Thank you for almost killing me. Why would I care to live in a world filled with such crass and uncaring people?"

The provost's long red eyebrows went up in delight. "Oh, did I scare you?"

"We would have gladly plunged through a railing," Jackie laughed, still trying to catch her breath.

"What have you found out so far?" Ashley smiled delightedly.

"That I . . ."—Quest unsteadily got to his feet—" . . . am too old for this nonsense. Why I permitted you to drag me into the one homicide on record that does not somehow involve the Communications Department, I'll never know. I shan't, I assure you, make that particular mistake again."

Going as quickly as his spindly legs could carry him, Chairman Quest moved toward the door. "Ashley, dear. She's all yours. If you're not willing to do it, we'll just have to wait until Algie sobers up. Cheerio."

As the gasping director left, Ashley and Jackie shared a laugh. "Sorry," Ashley said warmly, holding Jackie's arm. "I just couldn't resist."

"I would have done the same thing," Jackie laughed. "Sorry to admit it."

"Yes, but you're ten years younger than I am," Ashley continued in her beautiful low voice. "I'm the president of the distinguished Rodgers University Board. I have to stop acting like I'm still playing with Barbie dolls."

"You have to have some fun," Jackie smiled. She really liked Ashley Landis who was quite down to earth, though Jackie knew she was very likely a millionaire.

The dean provost returned her smile. "So what has Palmer's premiere amateur sleuth discovered so far?"

"Not much," Jackie confessed. "I can see this was all carefully planned. The murderess . . ."

"Uh oh," Ashley interrupted. "Stop right there. Why murderess?"

"Well, the voice."

"Somebody doing what I just did?"

"Yes," Jackie replied. "Or whatever."

Ashley threw her arms up in irritation. "Oh, come on, Jackie. How hard was that? Half the campus—male, female, young, and old—could do it. And you don't even have to use a lady's voice in this case. Yell, 'Boo!' or whisper, 'I'm going to kill you,' and you'll scare the sugar out of someone."

"No doubt, but . . ." Jackie fidgeted, pressing the skin on one knuckle, then just coming out with it. "Well, I didn't want to say it—but at the risk of sounding like a female chauvinist, this whole crime seems too devious to be the work of a man."

"I agree completely," Ashley said at once. "Let's go downstairs. I'll show you where he went splat."

CHAPTER 3

A few hours later Jackie was at home, dressed in a more comfortable russet-brown sweater and blue jeans. As she fed her loyal dog his dinner, she remarked, "Pretty grim, Jake. They had this horrible foam that they now spray to give a three-dimensional view of the corpse position. It looked like one of the pod people. In fact, I should screen *Invasion of the Body Snatchers* in the lab tomorrow. That's still one of the scariest . . ."

All of a sudden there was a crashing noise. Jackie jumped. Peter Walsh, her troublesome eleven-year-old, lurched into the room. "Ma! Guess what?"

"You forgot how many stairs there were again and crashed into the wall?" Jackie guessed.

"I don't think so," Peter replied. "Listen, Mom. You know that tape you told me I should watch?"

Jackie put the big clip back on the *Deluxe Doggie Gobbles* and guessed, "Miss Manners?"

Peter positively throbbed with disgust. "The radio station tape."

"From three months ago?"

"Whatever."

"Okay," Jackie led her son into the den area of her living room. "What did you discover, my beautiful sweet child?"

"Well," Peter said shyly. "I think I know who did it."

Jackie nodded, went to a red leather photo album on her desk, and showed Peter the last page. "Was it this man, here pictured on the front page of the *Herald* under the headline, 'Murderer Plunges to His Death'?"

"Uh . . . yeah."

Jackie looked at her son for a moment, then, with the tiniest of smiles, averred, "I love you, Peter."

"Yeah, well, ditto, Mom."

"Can you spare a hug?"

Peter embraced his mother. He was almost as tall as she was. Jackie picked a piece of food off his chest.

"Yum. Pop-Tarts. Ready for a real meal?"

"Yeah, if it isn't fish." Peter followed his mother back into the kitchen. "Mom . . ."

"Yes, dear?" Jackie took the broiled halibut out of the oven with protective mitts and, shielding it with her body, carefully covered every inch of the fish with onion rings.

"Mom! Are you listening to me?"

"Of course I am, my darling. What is it?"

"You sound like grandma."

"Sorry. What is it, my little four-leaf clover?"

Peter toyed with his spoon, sending a lightbulb-shaped pepper shaker crashing to the floor. "You didn't forget it's my birthday in September?"

"How could I forget the twelfth anniversary of the longest night of my life?" Jackie asked with feigned wide-eyed surprise.

"I guess. Anyway, Mom . . ."

Jackie scooped some halibut on her own plate, hoping that her son would not see the connection. "Yes, Peter precious?"

Peter followed his mother over to the table and sat down. Seeing that there was a glass of milk laid out for him, he quickly poured it into Jake's dish and got himself a root beer from the refrigerator.

"Peter. Do you want Jake to get worms?" Jackie poured herself a glass of Goodwillie water from a gallon dispenser. "If you don't want milk, say so. Don't just throw it away."

"Sorry," Peter yelled.

It was all right. Jake merely pushed his bowl to a well-ventilated corner where the milk could be left to sour. The canny canine knew that sour milk was often just the thing for scrubbing oil stains out of carpets.

Peter picked up the pepper shaker, placed it back on the table, and then sat heavily, causing the napkin holder to plunge off the other side of the table. Unconcerned, he resumed his conversation with his mother. "Listen. Can I ask you something?"

Jackie sat down, beamed at her dish, and then delicately unfolded her napkin. "Yes. As soon as your mouth is empty again."

Peter chewed his first bite of food with exaggerated thoroughness. "Hey, you know this isn't bad. What is it?"

"Peacock," Jackie lied.

"No kidding?"

Jackie carefully pushed a casserole dish toward Peter. "Have some green beans."

He pushed them right back. "Bleah."

"You liked them Monday."

"They had cheese and stuff on 'em. Listen. What's the deal with that Ron guy?"

Jackie shrugged. "As far as I know he doesn't have any cheese on him."

Peter wiped his face with his hand the way Brian Keith used to do on *Family Affair*. "I mean . . . are you two guys, you know?"

"Dating? Yes."

"Good," Peter went over and shoveled the last of his food onto the spot where Jake's bowl usually reposed. "Don't drop him until after Christmas."

"Hey, there's a plan. You counting on an expensive gift?"

Peter scratched Jake's neck as the big dog finished off the last of his alleged peacock dinner. "When we go out there. You know, for Christmas vacation . . ."

"Yes?" Jackie was only half-listening as she watched the dog eat the fish and hoped he would not choke on a bone.

"He's taking me to a Sharks hockey game. Ron. Sharks-Penguins."

"Those poor birds," Jackie commented, knowing it would infuriate her son.

"Ma! Don't be dumb! The Penguins will eat them for lunch."

"Wouldn't it be wonderful if you would eat more of your dinner, Peter?"

Jackie's only son made a distraught face. "I had a lot. That peacock starts out good, but ends up tasting like fish."

"About your father," Jackie changed the subject quickly.

"What about him?"

Jackie finished her own dinner and carried the plates over to the sink. "When I take you over there this weekend, I may want to talk to him."

This actually came close to intriguing Peter. "What for? My birthday? By the way, I think you guys should make a big deal, this time. I'm getting pretty old, you know."

"You and me both, pal," Jackie responded, bending down for the dishwasher soap. "And don't remind your father about your birthday either."

"Why not?" Peter asked, slouching down and moving the spilled napkins closer to himself by fishing them over with the toe of his sneaker. "What happened?"

Jackie massaged her lower back. "I've told you this story a hundred times."

"So what," Peter shrugged, putting his feet up on his mother's now empty chair. "Tell me again."

"Well," Jackie came over and dumped Peter's feet off. "In those days your father smoked." She then wiped off the chair and table with a damp Handi-wipe. "And he was nervous because I was in labor with you for so long."

Peter whooped. "What's the matter? Was he late for a golf game?"

Jackie held out her palm. Peter slapped it.

"Good one, hunh, Mom?"

"I don't know why people don't laugh out loud when they see you coming," Jackie assured her son.

"Anyway . . . ?"

Jackie put on the Mr. Coffee and sat back down. Jake resumed his usual spot under the table and Jackie put her feet up on him. "Anyway, your Dad kept running out to the parking lot to have another cigarette. Finally it started raining. And your Dad didn't want to get all wet, so he tried to open the window in the waiting room. But it was low, and it had been painted recently, so it got stuck. And your father, being your father, got flustered and tried to force it."

"And he broke the window?" Peter chuckled, anticipating a whole new ending to a much-told story.

"No. He fell out."

"Out the window?" asked an amazed Peter.

"Out the window . . ." Jackie confirmed. " . . . into the bushes and then rolled down the hill. Marx-Wheeler had to put up warning signs after that. 'Don't Fall Out the Window and Roll Down the Hill!' "

Peter laughed. "And Dad was really banged up, wasn't he?"

"To the max," Jackie laughed along with her son. "He sprained both his ankles and scraped himself up. He was in the hospital as long as you and me."

"That's great," Peter exclaimed.

"I don't know about great," Jackie responded, belatedly reining in her son's blood-thirstiness. "But I was the only new mother in the hospital who had to listen to her husband complain about *his* stitches."

Just then the phone rang.

Jackie rushed to get it. "Hello?"

"Ms. Walsh?" an unfamiliar voice demanded.

"Yes?" she replied, a little alarmed.

"This is Chief Healy of the Palmer police, university precinct."

"Yes?" Jackie remembered the tough former homicide captain who had retired and then returned to the police as chief of detectives because he missed the action.

"I wonder if I may speak with you, Ms. Walsh, about the death of Walter Hopfelt?"

"Well, of course, Chief Healy," Jackie's mind flew quickly to possible excuses. "I was just going out, though. I have an engagement."

"Well, I certainly don't want to interrupt that, Ms. Walsh," Healy replied with more than a touch of sarcasm. "How about if I give you a ride to where you're going and we can talk en route?"

Jackie considered that. While she sort of liked the idea of riding in a police car, the drawback, obviously, was that she would have to take a dispatch cab back from her poker game. "Tell you what, Chief," she counterproposed. "Are you calling from your car?"

Jackie knew that the Palmer police, like most of their

big city counterparts, had replaced the old shortwave police radios with cellular phones.

"Yes."

"Is Felix Cruz with you?" Jackie also knew that the bright Dominican homicide detective had chosen not to follow the recently promoted Captain Michael McGowan back to the central precinct.

"Yes," Healy replied again.

"How about meeting me at my house?" Jackie suggested. "You can ride with me and Detective Sergeant Cruz can follow us."

Jackie could tell from the old chief's voice that he wasn't happy about the arrangement, but he agreed, telling her he'd be there in five minutes. As Jackie put her cordless phone back on its recharging pad, she made an impetuous decision. "Peter!"

Jackie's son appeared at once.

Feeling a motherly rush of love for her red-haired darling, Jackie put her arms around Peter and gave him a hard squeeze. "I love you, do you know that?"

"I've heard it said," Peter replied enigmatically.

Jackie made a Gale Storm face, which eventually broke up her almost twelve-year-old. "Do you think you can stay here alone tonight? I won't be home too late."

"Sure, why not?"

"Good," Jackie smiled. "I'd leave you with the Cooks, but they had to go out this evening."

"I know. Isaac's my friend, remember?"

Jackie sighed. Did everyone have to treat her like she was the stupidest person on earth? "Yes, dear. I remember. Now, I'll be home around twelve. I expect to find you sound asleep."

Peter groaned as if harpooned. "Mom, it's *summer*!"

"You're going back to school in four days."

"I hate school."

"So do I," Jackie readily confessed. "But I have to teach it and you have to attend it."

Peter responded in one of Jackie's least favorite ways—by sticking his finger down his throat.

"Listen." Jackie held Peter's chin in her fingers. "You stay home tonight. No walks to the store. You keep the doors locked. No visitors."

"Why?" Peter demanded. "What are you worrying about?"

Jackie decided to level with him. "There is some disturbed person out there who killed Mr. Hopfelt at the university. And we're going to be careful until that person is caught and put in jail."

"Do you think it's that woman who they let out of jail?" Peter asked suddenly.

Jackie looked into her son's eyes. "I don't know, Peter. But I think it may well be."

Lorne Healy, a thick, beetle-browed, career police officer who had disarmed and subdued three of Palmer's most fearsome criminals using his bare hands, a blinding handful of powdered sugar, and a jumbo thermos of coffee, did not bother to pretend even for a moment to like being driven around by a woman. Especially a woman who was notorious for driving as if the streets of Palmer were the Indianapolis Speedway.

"If . . ." the red-faced chief of detectives sputtered, "you go through one more red light, I am going to impound this vehicle and throw you in jail. Do you understand me?"

Easing her foot a little on the gas pedal, Jackie replied, "I'm terribly sorry, Chief. Did that last light turn before I got through the intersection?"

"Never mind that," Healy barked. "What can you tell me

about Hopfelt? Did he have any enemies?"

For the first time in years, Jackie came to a full stop at a stop sign. "Enemies?" Jackie considered for a moment, her foot beating a tattoo on the accelerator. "I don't know. He wasn't well liked. I don't even know if he was married."

Healy shook his head. "He wasn't."

"I didn't think so." Jackie started the car forward again, took a deep breath, then decided to go for broke. "Have you considered the possibility, Chief, that this murder may be related to another murder at the college?"

Healy made a face, not knowing whether or not Jackie was making fun of him. "Because there have been so *many* murders at the college, do you mean?"

"You know, Chief," Jackie responded easily. "I don't know if I've ever shared this theory with you before, but I think this may be related in some fundamental way to Hiroshima."

"Hopfelt was killed by Japs, you mean?"

"No, Chief," Jackie responded seriously. "The large number of murders at the college. And in the world in general. I firmly believe that after the atom bomb was exploded and everyone realized that we actually had the capability to end all existence, to blow the planet to pieces, that it changed people." Jackie threaded a path between two cars that most people would have been reluctant to try to walk through. "The knowledge that we had the seeds of eternal destruction in our hands somehow made everything a little bleaker. It changed the quality of human life. It cheapened it somehow and made it less of a crime against nature to commit individual murders, when a few men in power had the ability, any time they chose to use it, to kill everyone. To murder the world, as it were."

Healy gave Jackie a dark look. "Could we please get back to the affairs of Walter Hopfelt?"

"Yes, Chief. I'm sorry. What did you want to ask?"

Healy clenched his teeth as Jackie avoided waiting for a light by cutting across a recycling lot. "You were saying that the death of Hopfelt may have been related to another murder. Danielle Sherman, I assume."

Jackie nodded, rolled down her window, and hooked an aluminum can neatly into the appropriate receptacle. "I can't prove it yet, but yes, that's what I think."

"Because the dummy that scared Hopfelt to death was found wearing her jacket?"

"Yes, Chief, I was going to ask. Well . . ."

"You were going to ask your pal Mike McGowan to re-open the Danielle Sherman investigation," Healy supplied.

"You heard."

"Word gets around," Healy responded with heavy sarcasm. "Well, it's not up to McGowan anymore. It's up to me now."

"I know," Jackie said slowly. She then turned to the gruff detective. "How about it?"

Healy clearly wasn't happy to be reminded of the case that led to his temporary ouster. "It's a black eye to me personally."

Jackie nodded. "I'm just a film instructor, Chief Healy. I'm not trying to tell you how to do your job."

Healy rubbed his face roughly with his hand. "I'm a public servant, Ms. Walsh. You have the right to criticize my performance. You pay my salary."

"So?"

"Suppose I say . . . yes?"

Jackie felt a thrill go through her.

"You realize, of course," Healy continued, "that a lot of people will think that this is just a vindictive act to get Merida Green?"

Jackie nodded. "I do realize that."

"So?"

"Maybe we have a right to be vindictive," Jackie answered quietly. "A young girl was killed." Jackie then slowed to signal the police car behind her she that was preparing to make a right turn, then hung a ricky into the parking lot of the Strang Apartment Complex, where her mother lived.

"The girl . . ." Healy began.

"Danielle," Jackie supplied somewhat impatiently.

Healy ground his teeth. He hated to be shown up. "I recall she was killed by a hypodermic needle pushed into her heart."

"Not the way most people do drugs," Jackie pointed out, pulling the Jeep into the parking lot.

"There's a reason for that," Healy continued. He then stopped to wipe his face again. "You have got to be strong to push a 10 cc needle through a person's breast bone. The pathologist who did the autopsy says she wasn't strong enough to do it herself."

"Well, Cosmo Gordon would know," Jackie remarked as she cruised through the lot looking for a parking spot. "Too bad he's out of town."

"Actually, I wasn't referring to Dr. Gordon," Healy responded. "He didn't do the actual autopsy. Dr. Humphries of his department did. She's the acting M.E. and she's willing to swear that the needle was pushed into the chest from an angle that is inconsistent with suicide. And . . ."

"And . . . ?" Jackie prompted.

"The person was strong. Strong and probably left-handed."

"I don't know, but Merida Green has always struck me as being physically strong," Jackie said quickly.

Healy nodded, and then continued reading from his notes. "Dr. Humphries thinks it was a man, Jackie. A left-handed man. A left-handed man like Walter Hopfelt."

Healy looked into Jackie's face. Their eyes locked for several moments and then she asked, "How strong is the evidence?"

"That's all there is," Healy rasped. "It wouldn't be enough to convict Hopfelt if he was on trial. But the original detectives on the case, John Mason and Buchanan Bendix . . ."

Jackie immediately formed a mental picture of the tall square-jawed men, whom she had first met briefly while investigating the murder of a dog breeder named Mel Sweeten last year.

" . . . recall that Hopfelt did hang around the Blue Jay. His statement at that time indicates he used to go over there to chase college kids out of the place so they wouldn't get into trouble. No one had any reason to doubt it, but . . ." Healy let it hang.

"What motive would he have for killing Danielle?" Jackie asked.

"The same one the Green woman had. That the girl knew he killed Philip Barger."

Jackie shook her head, perplexed. "But Danielle's midterm paper. It named Merida Green. That's why she stole it from my office."

"Merida Green didn't have a key to your office," Healy remarked quietly. "Walter Hopfelt did. We've never found that paper, Jackie. We don't know what it said."

"But the ashes were found in her office."

"By Walter Hopfelt," Healy pointed out. "And for whatever it's worth, Merida Green denied she ever saw the paper. She denies she destroyed it. The worst part is, we don't know what information the girl had. She may have heard that Merida Green had a grudge against Philip Barger and assumed she killed him . . ."

"The way we did," Jackie interjected.

Healy nodded. "Suppose instead of trying to blackmail

Merida, which her family assured us she would have never done, little Danielle went to the university's security chief, Walter Hopfelt? And suppose Hopfelt took advantage of the girl's suspicions to pin the blame on Merida Green? Like with your Mr. Hopfelt, we don't know if she had any enemies, but she wasn't well liked."

Jackie sat back in her seat. She felt like getting out of her Jeep and walking around the parking lot, but she was just too overwhelmed. "I can't believe it wasn't her."

"I'm not sure Merida Green didn't kill Philip Barger, Ms. Walsh," Healy replied. "She certainly had a motive and as far as we know, Walter Hopfelt didn't. But Merida didn't try to break into your house the first time your dog chased someone away. She had an airtight alibi for that night. Hopfelt didn't."

"It leaves things more confused than ever," Jackie commented.

"It does indeed."

Healy, Jackie noticed, exhaled loudly after every sentence. She wondered if that bespoke an upcoming respiratory problem or simply a woeful outlook on life.

"What do you want me to do?" she asked finally.

"Go ahead and do your investigation," Healy decided. "You won't have to be as wary of politics as me. But I'm not like your friend McGowan. There's no way I'm going to let you go off and solve the case alone and then call me to show up at the end with a cocked gun and a new set of handcuffs. If there's an arrest to be made, I'll make it alone. You may decide you know who did it, and I may decide you're wrong or that we need more evidence before we go public with it." Healy then became aware of Jackie's critical look and raged, "Don't look at me like that. I'm not worried about hogging credit. You can have all you want. I'm worried about your life, lady. You are not a cop. You don't have the department to protect you. You don't have weapons training . . ."

"Actually, I'm starting to practice with a pistol . . ."

"It's going to take more than that."

"I have Jake," Jackie said simply. "He's always kept me safe before."

"Maybe so," Healy nodded. "He's a good dog. He used to work for the department, I know. But he can't protect you from a lot of things. And if Merida Green is the murderer, the first thing she's going to do is plan a way to bypass Jake."

Jackie nodded at the truth of the remark. It made sense. After all, it was Jake who had knocked Merida Green down the first time she had tried to kill Jackie with a gun.

Healy had his hand on the door handle, but couldn't resist a parting shot. "Remember what happened to Hopfelt. He was a trained security man, presumably aware that his life might be in danger. He got a note, we figure, saying, 'Meet me.' Maybe somebody forges President Foreman's signature. Hopfelt goes up the stairs. A fright. A trip. A fall. A man's dead. Keep it in mind. You're a smart lady, but you're just as easy to kill as the rest of us."

CHAPTER 4

Once a week, as long as Jackie could remember, Frances Costello, her spry, henna-haired mother, hosted a poker party. The plastic poker chips in the shamrock-shaped holder would come out, the extensions would go into the round living room table, and Frances would turn to the next page in her John Scarne cookbook and prepare the most delicious poker snacks this side of Monte Carlo.

Still mulling over what the chief had said to her, Jackie took the elevator to the lucky seventh floor and let herself into her mother's apartment with her key.

"Ah, Jackie, love," Frances smiled as she came in. She then took off her orange dealer's eyeshade so it wouldn't bruise her daughter's forehead when they kissed. "How are you, my darling?"

"I'm okay. Sorry I'm late, everyone." Jackie smiled apologetically at the other players. Seated next to Frances was Bara Day, a tough-talking former night nurse whom her mother had met at Al-Anon. The two women, roughly the same age, had independently come up with the same way of handling their eventual widowhood. They had bought big snakes.

Bara had favored an anaconda at first, but eventually, tired of the big snake's big moods and financially straitened by continually having to replace the neighborhood pets, she had switched over to pythons like Jackie's mother.

The last few years, Bara and Frances had gotten into the habit of buying their snakes at the same time. Bara would always get a female. Frances would always get a male. Bara's current beauty was a light gray rock python with spoon-shaped white spots named Scalia. Frances's snake, a big, sinuous black jungle python named Victor, had developed a marked fondness for the two-hundred-pound minx and the two women were hoping that one Thursday night the inevitable would happen and they would become serpent grandmothers—in a manner of speaking.

Seated next to Bara was Jean Scott, the bright, white-haired book reviewer for the *Herald-Chronicle* and an old family friend. Jean—who had actually been closer to Jackie's father Pete in his lifetime—was Jackie's biggest fan when it came to her writing.

Somehow, although Jean Scott's tastes ran to Jane Austen, whenever she read something Jackie wrote, even something as trivial as a half-hour situation comedy script, the veteran book reviewer could always put her finger on whatever needed to be changed or improved. At home, among her books, plants, and cats (Snoozle and Forbes), Jean was a picture of calm, grandmotherly wisdom. Here, playing poker, she smoked like a chimney, cursed like a sailor, and was known to drink as many as three boilermakers in a single evening.

Next to Jean was Milly Brooks, a petite brunette with big hair. A friend of Jackie's since childhood (they met at the school nurse's office and discovered, much to each other's delight, that they both liked Vicks), Milly taught in the English Department at Rodgers. Milly and Jackie had started at the university at about the same time, but Milly had kept her job while Jackie quit for about ten years to stay home with her family. Now, whenever Jackie needed to know something about what was happening in the university outside of her own insular Communications Department, Jackie relied on her friend Milly.

In the eight months or so that Milly had been coming to the game, she had developed a fascinating series of quirks and tics, which, along with her constant gum cracking, so distracted her fellow players that the diminutive Sex in Literature instructor often ended up one of the game's big winners.

Last in the circle, and beautiful, although wearing a T-shirt and jeans instead of her usual silk suits and power sports outfits, was Suki Tonawanda, playing in her first game. Suki, a slim, lovely, tallish Asian-American with casually laquered hair and an ironic smile, taught film studies along with Jackie at the university. More a dialogue director than a writer, Suki had been Jackie's assistant for two years and then had graduated to full-instructor status.

Jackie was proud of her. Although the young woman occasionally confided her insecurities to Jackie during curriculum meetings, Jackie had never seen Suki falter before a group of students.

Obviously happy to see her friend, Suki called out a cheery, "Hey, Jackie!"

"Hi, Sook," Jackie smiled. "This band of robbers cheating you blind?"

Suki nodded. "I had a mink coat when I came here."

"Just be glad you're wearing underwear, dear," Frances commented.

"Mother!" Jackie exclaimed.

"How do you know I'm wearing underwear?" Suki asked.

"Don't let these tinted spectacles fool you, darling . . ."

Jackie interrupted her mother to crack, "Those glasses are infrared, Suki. And of course the cards are marked . . ."

Milly, although she knew that her friend was probably kidding, nonetheless folded her cards and covered them with her hands.

"If I may," Frances continued with queenly dignity, "I was about to say that my eyes are still strong enough to see panty lines through the tight pants that you girls wear. In my day, and of course I wouldn't dream of being critical . . ."

Jean Scott started coughing and Frances gave her a narrow look, wondering whether it was the carbon monoxide from the elderly reviewer's cigarettes or if her long-ago rival for the affections of John Peter Costello was pretending to choke with disbelief.

" . . . we wore petticoats to avoid even the wildest suspicion of such a thing," Frances continued, somewhat nettled.

Suki, embarrassed to have her lingerie become the subject of conversation, was looking for a joke she could use to change the subject, when Bara Day beat her to the punch.

"What the hell are you going on about, you old bat! The only reason we hid our waistband lines was because in our day it would have meant we were wearing a girdle. Now get your ante where it should be and try to concentrate on what I'm dealing you all. The game is seven card stud. If you don't have a stud in your life, it's good that you have two extra cards, anyway."

Kicking off her shoes with a smile, Jackie settled back to enjoy the card game.

The evening passed quickly. Although all concerned had a good time, the night didn't get quite as hilarious as usual because of the news that Frances's good friend, Maggie Mulcahy, an original poker regular, was in the hospital.

Jackie offered Suki a ride home and they had a good talk while the powerful, candy-apple red Jeep motored through the semideserted weeknight streets.

"I love your mother's friend," Suki commented. "What is her name?"

"Bara," Jackie responded.

"She's so funny."

"I like her too."

"What was that she was saying about feeding her snake only white mice?"

" 'Always feed it something the color you ain't' I believe was the quote."

Suki laughed all over again. "Well, I enjoyed that, thank you."

"I hope you'll come again."

"I'd love to." Suki checked out her eyebrows in the mirror on the reverse side of the passenger sun visor, then slyly changed the subject. "So, word is, you're out for Merida Green's hide."

Jackie breathed deeply, gripped the steering wheel a little tighter with her glove-clad hands, and then said, "I don't think I want to talk about that."

Suki knew Jackie well enough to persist gently. "I don't think she killed Danielle, you know? Phil Barger, sure. But I don't think she killed Brown Eyes."

"Is that what they called her?" Jackie asked in a soft voice.

"It's what I called her," Suki responded equally softly. "I don't think that Merida would kill Danielle a different way than she killed Philip Barger."

Jackie shrugged. She had thought of that too. Many times. "It was pretty widely publicized. The way Philip Barger died. You'd have to be pretty silly indeed to sit down to a cup of tea with her."

Suki shook her head impatiently. "It wouldn't have to be done face to face, Jackie. Danielle drank tons of McKean Carrot Soda. Everyone knew that."

"Would that mask the taste of cyanide?" Jackie asked.

"It would mask the taste of gasoline," Suki replied.

Jackie made the appropriate face.

"And another thing," Suki persisted.

"Must we?"

"I'm sorry. I know I'm being rude—taking advantage of your hospitality this way to tell you things you don't want to hear. It's just that . . ." Suki gave her friend a wan smile. " . . . Jackie you are, like, well, not a mom—you're not old enough for that, and I have a great mom—but like a big sister. A really good-friend-big-sister, and I don't want to see you go out on a limb and maybe get fired from the university."

"I don't think that will happen," Jackie responded, a little taken aback.

"You don't know."

"Suki," Jackie raised her voice to be heard over the snores of her hardworking dog, now fast asleep on the backseat. "The U is behind me on this one. Really. Chairman Quest, Provost Landis, President Foreman all asked me to . . . well, you know, do my thing with Jake and see what I can find out."

"Jackie!" Suki bent forward, touched her friend's knee and said very earnestly, "Maybe they don't know. Being academics and all . . ."

"Ivor Quest is hardly an academic, Suki."

"But he's hardly familiar with Palmer politics either."

"And you are?"

Suki withdrew, obviously hurt by the remark. When she had leaned back as far away from Jackie as she could get in the small vehicle, Suki responded, "As a matter of fact, I am. My father owns a restaurant, you know, where all the politicians eat. He knows Big Bill Curtis. They've been friends, to some extent, for thirty years. Bill Curtis may not be the mayor of this town any more, but he is still very powerful. He doesn't want his daughter's case re-opened. It's officially a suicide. That's it."

"Here we are," was Jackie's only remark, as the Jeep pulled up in front of Suki's apartment building.

"Thank you." The two women sat in the car for a moment, looking straight out the window. "I'm sorry, Jackie."

"I'm sorry too, Suki."

"I just don't want . . ."

"I know. Believe it or not, Suki," Jackie added, "this is not a vendetta. It's just that I have to live in this town. My son has to live here and so do my mother and my friends. I can't sleep at night if I know there's a murderer on the loose and I can do something to put him or her away and I'm not doing anything about it."

"Please be careful."

"I will," Jackie promised. "Listen, I can sympathize with someone losing a child. I don't know what I would do if what happened to Danielle happened to Peter. But I couldn't live with myself if I didn't know."

Suki nodded.

Jackie continued, "I don't know Bill or Elizabeth Curtis, but I think they would sleep better at night if they knew what really happened to their beautiful daughter."

"You're a big girl, I guess," Suki replied sadly.

"I wouldn't go that far," Jackie smiled. Then, before Suki could get out, Jackie grabbed her arm.

"What?"

"Isn't that place where Danielle—isn't the Blue Jay around here somewhere?"

"Right up the block," Suki nodded. "Only it's called Circus Maximus now."

Jackie squinted into the street lights and saw in the distance a big blue neon sign hovering above an overly lit parking lot. "Feel like checking it out?"

"I've checked it out, Jackie," Suki replied disgustedly. "It's a dump. Honest. And dangerous. A girl I went to high school with was dragged into a van in the parking lot. Really messed up. She hasn't been the same since."

Jackie would not be dissuaded. "What if I get reinforcements?"

"The cops?"

"Better than that."

CHAPTER 5

Bara Day arrived in her Volkswagen Land Cruiser no more than twenty minutes later. With her in the gray van was Frances Costello, the peppy Jake, and Scalia, the drowsy river python who had been teased into a large letter "D" by Jackie's faithful canine companion.

"Thanks for coming, Mom," Jackie said, leaning in the open passenger side window to kiss her mother on the cheek.

"Well, it's about time you invited your mother along on one of your wild adventures," Frances replied. She then flung open her door, making Jackie jump back to avoid being hit. "Now if one of us gets hurt with a knife or something we have a nurse along. If you can call this one a nurse."

Bara, slowly working her way out of her shoulder harness was quick to reply, "I'm as a good a nurse now as I ever was."

"No one's arguing with you on that score, Bara," Frances replied, rolling her eyes to amuse her daughter. "Give me your hand, will you love? This knee doesn't like to step down anymore."

Jackie helped her mother alight from the van. "Well, it was nice of you *both* to come."

Frances nodded, then noticed Suki for the first time.

"Jacqueline Shannon, what are you doing dragging this little girl along with you? You should be home in bed, young lady."

"My boyfriend will keep the sheets warm till I get there," Suki responded with a wink.

Frances narrowed her eyes. "Oh, it's like that, is it?"

"I'm afraid so," Suki smiled. "Klaus and I have been living together for almost three years."

"Not Klaus Klingelhoffer, the baker's son?"

Suki was amazed. "You know Klaus?"

"I do indeed," Frances responded. "Bounced him on my knee when he was a lad and my damn knee joint worked the way it should. Well, I'm surprised, I must say."

"Mother . . ."

"Don't get me wrong," Frances protested. "It's not that I disapprove. You can be sure I was doing me best to get handsome boys in my bed from the day I graduated high school."

"Mother . . ."

"Biology embarrasses my daughter," Frances replied, pinching Jackie's cheek. "It's probably why she never got good grades in science all through school. Anyway, Snooky . . ."

"Suki, Mother!" Jackie hissed.

"Suki, then! I thought she was named after Fanny Brice. What's the shame in that?"

Jackie was happy to see Suki giggling instead of stomping off.

"What I was saying," Frances continued blithely, "is that things were different when I was a girl. We lived at home as long as we could. Not out of any moral principle, you understand, but because it was cheaper. You could still do the wild thing if that's what you and your beau wanted, but it also gave the lad a chance to work and save for a few years and for people to get used to the idea that you were gonna get married and would be needing a wedding gift. So, by the time you were ready to set up housekeeping together you had some money in the bank and the woman didn't have to work."

"I see the advantage," Suki conceded. "My mother tells me that it's only because women had to go to work that TV's gotten so bad."

"Your mother sounds like a very nice woman," Frances said at once. "I'd like to meet her."

All of a sudden, Bara Day appeared in the van's sliding door with Scalia wrapped around her waist.

"Here you are," Frances remarked. "I thought you'd keeled over of a stroke in there, and of course I can't drive a stick shift."

"It's not a stick shift, you ancient crone. It's an automatic! How many times have you ridden with me to the Snake Club? Would you please get your eyes checked before you walk into an open manhole or something?" Bara slid her fingers gently down the neck of her snake and got a big fangy smile as her reward.

"What are you doing?" Frances asked. "Bringing her inside?"

"Yup."

"Well, I'm sure there's a law against that," Frances fretted.

"Hell, there's laws against half the things these young folks is doin' in there. So let the kids break the law their way and I'll break the law mine. Speaking of kids," Bara transitioned, laying eyes for the first time on Suki, "what are you doing still up, child?"

"Oh, don't worry about her," Frances interjected. "She's sleeping with Klingelhoffer's boy. So she's got no cause to worry."

"Oh," Bara exclaimed loudly. It was fortunate for her snake that he was stone deaf and thus impervious to his mistress's loud voice. "So you're rolling in dough, hunh? Well, don't let him give you any damn prenuptial agreement."

"Actually," Suki smiled. "If you count my parents' restaurant, real estate, and take-out One Stop business, I'm probably worth more than he is."

"Well, don't for Pete's sake let *him* know that," Bara instructed. "Keep two sets of books. Always keep a man in the dark about how much money you have. What a husband doesn't know won't hurt him."

"I hate to break all this merriment up," Jackie interrupted. "But the Circus is only open until four in the morning."

The management of the Circus Maximus did everything in their power to fool people into thinking they were having a good time. Once a year in August, because there weren't any good real holidays to tie a series of special expensive mixed drinks to, the Circus had a two-week festival, which they called "Circus Time at the Circus!"

During this festive period, the staff dressed in outrageous circus outfits and the patrons were encouraged, at their own expense and inconvenience of course, to dress like clowns as well.

Jackie and her party paid their way in and were dazzled by the show.

Canvas had been stretched across the dark ceiling to give the illusion of being in a big top. Three fluorescent rings had been painted on the floor and waitresses garbed like trapeze artists walked around the club, holding trays and boxes of festive drinks in balloon-decorated paper cups. The bouncers, an oafish lot led by former Palmer High wrestling stars, were dressed as strongmen, complete with red and black striped shirts, derbies, and waxed handlebar mustaches. The house band, appropriately, wore baggy pants and other comic garb, and Bud Brown, the lead singer, positively swam in a pair of enormous checkered trousers held up by Day-Glo yellow suspenders.

The regular crowd, drinkers, swingers, and people who just couldn't help moving to the music, moved carefully across the slick, sawdust-covered floor dressed as gymnasts, star dancers, blue-winged bats, and other striking creatures of the night. Even the older men, married mostly, who came to ogle the younger women, wore festive bow ties or jeweled, trained-seal ornaments on their inevitable gold neck chains.

Pushing through a group of patrons wearing lorgnette masks, fake furs, and genuine feather boas, Jackie's party passed the slack wire that had been run between two posts over a muddy Jell-O pit. A daring few, some in aerialist tights, took their chances and awkwardly jumped the pit. The other activities the Circus had scheduled for the evening included *Loop the Loop* (in a shopping basket), toss your coins in the festive tips pitcher, and throw the dwarf in the ringmaster suit onto the Velcro wall. First-aid people were attending to one game little fellow as Jackie found a table for her party. Although she marveled at the colorful dress of her fellow Palmerites, Jackie felt, as she usually did, that it was just too bad that people didn't go to more movies, see more theater, read more great books, or stay home more to converse with their loved ones. What was the point, after all, of living your life to impress waiters, bartenders, and maître d's?

Suddenly, she saw a familiar face. "Bill!"

"Jackie!" Putting down his chainsaw (apparently much to his boxed sister's audible relief), Bill Reigert, of Bill and Lil, Twin Magicians, abandoned his act and rushed to kiss Jackie's outstretched hand.

Charmed but determined not to show it, Jackie performed introductions.

"Bill Reigert, this is Suki Tonawanda, my friend from the university, my mother Frances Costello, and her friends Bara Day and Scalia the snake."

"Ladies," Bill nodded. "Snake. I see," he said, directing his comments to Bara Day who now had Scalia draped over her shoulders, "that you've decided to come in costume."

"Just don't pull any white rabbits out of the hat in front of this old girl," Bara warned.

"I certainly shall not." Reigert then turned to Jackie. "Could you be lovelier?" he gushed in his best mock-English accent.

"Oh, sure," Jackie responded honestly. In truth, it had been a long day and Jackie was drooping just about everywhere. "You've gone magically blond."

Reigert brushed a hand negligently though his long blond locks. "We both have. Lil and I. Right Lil?"

"Whatever you say, Bill," responded his boxed sister.

"After all," Bill continued loudly, suddenly remembering that he was, after all, in the middle of his magic act, "we are *twin* magicians."

A couple of barflies, dimly recognizing a cue, put down their bourbon-soaked cracker jacks and alcoholic cotton candy to applaud. Briefly.

"Thank you!"

"Oh, Bill!" the boxed Lil was, sad to say, sounding a bit peeved. "I hate to be a nudge, but . . ."

"Arise my sister, from your box of pain!" Reigert made a sweeping hand gesture and the locks on the magical box flew open.

The crowd, what there was of it, greeted the appearance of the lovely Lil with tsunami waves of apathy. Jackie's party clapped however, and Bill turned to them and bowed deeply. As he left the stage to sit down at their table, the waitress, unasked, brought over a tray of drinks.

"What do you think?" Reigert asked.

"Not bad," Frances remarked. She was always fond of magic, ever since Orson Welles had picked her out of the audience so he could pluck a silver necklace out of her bosom.

"How's that done?" Suki asked pleasantly.

"Magnets on the inside operated by your sister?" Jackie guessed.

"Radio control bracelet halfway up my right arm," Bill admitted cheerfully. Reigert then stood up and yelled to the few patrons still standing around. "How did you like that one, folks?"

The applause was not deafening.

"No? If you don't like that, how about this?" Reigert raised his arm to the ceiling and twisted his wrist to activate the microwave transmitters in his forearm band. The waves carried straight up to the ceiling, where they activated a large cesium-powered electric eye into releasing the trapdoors of the giant ceiling boxes.

Suddenly, much to everyone's surprise, dozens and dozens of birds swooped down from the ceiling.

"Look, doves!" one drunk cried out shrilly.

"What are you, blind?" called out another. "Those aren't doves, they're . . ."

"Squeak!" a bird shrieked out hoarsely.

" . . . pigeons!"

"Great effect . . . *not!*" commented Jackie, ducking as a rat of the air flew near her. "Ow!" Turning to Bill Reigert, Jackie asked, "Do pigeons bite?"

"I don't think so," he responded.

Jackie noticed that Reigert was now speaking with his regular Indiana accent and that he was obviously disturbed. "You mean you don't know?" Jackie exclaimed. "You put a bunch of birds in the ceiling to drop down on people and you don't know?"

Reigert answered, "No," but Jackie didn't hear him.

"You really are dangerous," Jackie continued. "You and your sister should come with warning labels."

"No, damn it! I did not put a bunch of birds in the ceiling!" Reigert made a quick move with his cape to block a pigeon that was making a beeline for Jackie. "I wouldn't put anything live up there. They're supposed to be balloons. Two hundred balloons in colorful circus shapes that I spent four hours tying. I hate pigeons."

"You and me both, brother," Jackie responded.

"Hey, he's *my* brother!" Lil corrected, suddenly appearing next to Bill and grabbing his arm. "Who put those awful things . . . ?"

"No friend of ours!" Reigert responded quickly. "Watch it, Ms. Costello!"

Frances picked up a chair and batted an attacking winged rodent away.

"Nice shot!" Reigert cheered, paying off the waitress, who wanted the tab settled before she ran screaming into the night. Reigert then turned to Jackie. "You wouldn't have anything to do with this, Jackie?"

The frizzy-haired film instructor glared daggers at the handsome young illusionist. "Do you really think I would . . . ?"

"I'm not saying you're the perpetrator . . ." Reigert took a moment to knock a bird away from his head. "I'm saying this might have been engineered by someone who wants you off the trail. You are on the trail, aren't you?"

"Is it that obvious?" Jackie asked, putting her arm over

her head as a bird whizzed by. "Ow! Look, it tore my jacket. Watch out, Bara!"

"Don't worry," the elderly nurse said confidently, her arms crossed and not a hair out of place. "Scalia is protecting me."

"But she hasn't moved," Lil protested.

"She doesn't have to, child," Bara explained. "Big snakes give off vibes. Dogs, birds, cats, mice, bugs—when they sense Scalia's in the room, they leave fast."

Jackie pointed to the big snake, now perched a couple of feet over Bara's head, straddling the two speakers. "Look, Bara! What's he doing up there?"

"They can't hear," Bara explained, "but they love to feel the vibrations through their belly." As Bara proudly beheld her eleven-foot snake, Reigert struck himself on the forehead.

"Damn!"

"What?" Frances asked. "Don't tell us you're thirsty for a canned vegetable cocktail."

"No," Reigert snapped. "The vibrations . . ."

The women gave the young illusionist a blank stare.

"The vibrations!" Reigert repeated loudly. "From the music! That's what's driving them wild!"

"Turn it off!" Jackie yelled up toward the unseen deejays.

"They can't hear you," Reigert told her. "They're probably all hiding somewhere."

Lil reached into her prop sack and slapped a sharp steely object on the table. "Here, Bill. Take this knife. Now, look in the corner up there on the loft. See?!"

The others craned their necks and stared at the sound balcony, where a single black power cord, with a white ceramic tip plugged into a powerbox, could be briefly glimpsed in the corner.

"I thought of that, Lil," Reigert said regretfully, clucking as the python's tail snapped out like a bullwhip and knocked another pigeon out of the air. "I could hit it from here, no problem . . ."

Frances and Bara were suitably impressed. The cord was easily fifty feet away.

" . . . but the metal knife would keep the connection and maybe start a fire as well."

"Then I'll handle it," announced Jackie. Taking her trusty silver whistle out of her special pocket, Jackie blew two times and in a moment . . .

. . . Jake was through the door.

"Up the stairs, Jake!" Jackie called out, as Frances knocked another bird out of the air.

"Good shot, Mrs. Costello!" Lil cried out in approval.

"Yes, well, I'm glad I don't have a set of these chairs at home," Frances replied mopping her brow. "If I had to drag out heavy chairs like these every Thursday I'd be with me nose in the sod before you could yell, 'Friday!' "

When the valiant dog had reached the top of the staircase, Jackie yelled up to him, "Now jump, Jake! Onto the balcony!"

Before the words had left her mouth, the Alsatian had bounded through the air to come lightly down on the wrought-iron railing.

"Good dog, Jake!" Jackie exulted.

The elderly snake owners and the twin magicians all shook their heads in amazement as they applauded the cunning canine. Even the birds stared fixedly at their new enemy.

"Now pull the cord, Jake!"

The big dog looked around. There were cords aplenty all around him.

Jackie reddened with embarrassment. Like most owners of smart animals, she knew that when her loyal pet didn't deliver, it was because he didn't receive the right instruction.

"The power cord, Jake! The black one!"

The dog looked around, found the cord in question, hopped up on a stool, and then pulled the plug with his teeth.

"Smart dog!" Reigert approved.

"Watch out!" As Jackie pointed, the others could see that the remaining birds had gathered themselves into an attack formation and were preparing to bombard Jake.

Jackie wasn't about to just stand around. She rushed for the special activity attractions at the far end of the dance floor.

As the dark-haired dog owner climbed the ladder to the Perilous Jump, Jake took cover between two of the largest lighting standards shining down on the dance floor.

Finally in place, Jackie grabbed the ornamental trapeze, hoping that it was firmly secured, brushed the stuffed Peggy Hippo doll off, and then took a deep breath.

"I used to be good at acrobatics in school," she told herself . . .

Fortunately, she was right above the Jell-O pit when she fell.

Jackie passed out for a moment, the breath knocked out of her. When she awoke, she saw the faces of her mother, Bara Day, and Bill Reigert looking down at her with concern. Bill's face seemed to swim a little and metamorphose into something entirely different. Then Jackie realized it was Lil standing over her, holding a plastic cup of some soapy amber liquid. "Drink this, Jackie."

Jackie made a face.

"Don't worry, it's light beer."

Jackie took the glass and drank deeply. "Jake . . . How is Jake?"

Lil brought over the happy dog who licked Jackie's cheek. Jackie knew it was affection and concern that motivated Jake, not the Jell-O that was all over her face. She responded by giving her dog a big hug. "How are you, boy?"

Reigert pointed with an elegant gesture to a covered garbage can. "I'll have you know he grabbed those last six birds and put them in that basket without ruffling a feather."

Reigert was starting to explain that there was a certain place on the arched spine of a pigeon that when gripped firmly paralyzes the wings, yet doesn't really hurt the bird, when Jackie passed out again.

CHAPTER 6

Jackie awoke in a kingsize bed with gray satin sheets.

"What was that?" she asked, dazed.

"Well, it was either an unfortunate accident," Bill Reigert answered, "or a brilliantly staged practical joke. Do you think someone's trying to tell you something, Jackie?"

"I have no idea," Jackie replied crossly. "What's in the glass?"

"Papaya juice. A miracle restorative for people who've suffered concussions. Or so it says on the bottle."

"Give."

Reigert put the glass firmly in Jackie's hand. She took a long hungry gulp and gave the three-quarters-empty glass to Reigert.

"How long have I been out?"

Reigert flicked his fingers. A pocket watch appeared in his hand and he consulted it. "About twelve hours. The doctor abandoned you to our tender ministrations. He seemed disappointed that you didn't need some terribly costly operation. But he did leave you a prescription for some ruinously expensive pharmaceuticals."

"So I'm okay," Jackie determined.

"Pretty much."

"Then why can't I feel my legs?"

Reigert gave a swift look downward. "Your long, shapely

gams are hopelessly entangled in my sheets."

"Oh."

"Allow me the privilege of untangling you."

Jackie watched the handsome illusionist move to the bottom of the bed. In a moment her legs were free and then she felt a soft whisper on the soles of her feet. "Now what are you doing?"

The pressure on her feet became delightfully stronger.

"Foot massage," Reigert purred. "A requisite in cases such as yours—I have it on good authority. I saw *Random Harvest* at least six times."

Tingles swept through Jackie. She liked *Random Harvest* a great deal herself. "Who undressed me and put me in this bed, Bill Reigert?"

"Your mother and her friend, unfortunately," Reigert replied with a wink. "Then we had to take two-hour shifts watching to see that you didn't start breathing funny."

"What do you mean?"

Reigert did a few Bert Lahr "nyah, nyahs" and then as Jackie laughed, he continued, "How would I know what a doctor means by breathing funny? So, for the last two hours I've sat here, watching you writhe erotically beneath these sheets."

Jackie's eyes narrowed. "I was probably dreaming of having pigeons peck my eyes out and you were getting turned on."

"I'm sorry," Reigert said at once. Tender and contrite, his silver-green eyes drew Jackie deep inside. "What could I have been thinking of? I'm wicked." Strong fingers crept up, massaging her ankles.

Jackie shifted on the mattress and said accusingly, "You're trying to seduce me, aren't you?"

"Of course I am," Reigert whispered.

"Well, you can't."

"Why not?"

"I have a headache."

They laughed for a long moment and the mood was broken.

"Would you like some aspirin?" Reigert offered.

"No, I think I just need some food. Oh, oh."

"What?" Reigert dropped Jackie's still tanned feet as if they were hot baked potatoes.

"Peter! Did anyone call my son?"

"Your mother did. I brought him over this afternoon."

"He's here? Now?"

"Right outside that door."

"Why?"

"It seems," Reigert answered casually, straightening up, "that it's his birthday."

"Oh, my goodness. That's right!"

Reigert splashed his hands with water from a washbowl and then carefully dried them with a fluffy hand towel decorated with stars and smiling half moons. "I could have gotten him some fabulous gift, but I didn't know whether you'd approve, and besides, on what my sister and I are making at the Circus Maximus these days, 'fabulous' is out of the question. So instead, your son and his friend Isaac are attending a command performance of an 'Afternoon of Captivating Illusions' as performed by 'Bill and Lil, Twin Magicians!' "

"Wow! When?"

Reigert looked at his watch. "Right now, as a matter of fact. You see, Lil and I sometimes exchange parts in the act. Hear the buzz of that chainsaw? Right now my dummy is being cut rather lustily into pieces."

Jackie looked at Reigert's kind face and felt a surge of gratitude.

"Thank you."

"My pleasure. How's that headache?"

"What headache?"

Reigert's move toward the bed was interrupted by a loud, cracking voice.

"Hi, Mom!" In a moment, her son was by her side. "You're up."

Jackie quickly drew her feet back under the sheets. "Uh, what I was . . ." She then looked around and saw that Reigert was gone. *Right*, she thought to herself. *He does that for a living, doesn't he?*

"Ma! You ain't talking to yourself, are you?" Peter asked worriedly.

"I am fine, my little twelve-year-old." Jackie reached out and pulled Peter to her chest. "How's your birthday so far?"

"Great! Grandma made pan pizza, Aunt Bara gave me a belt made out of real snake shedding and Doc Bellamy told me all about spinal fluid."

"Cool!"

"Mom, can I get a tattoo?"

"Of course not."

"Do I ever get anything I want on my birthday?!" Peter petulantly kicked at the base of the bed and in so doing accidentally broke the papaya juice glass.

"Apparently not. How about the magic show?"

"It's okay. It's still going on. You want to see it?"

"Peter!" Jackie pushed her son off the bed. "That show is being put on for you. Go back out there."

"What about you? Are you just going to sleep all day?"

"No, I'm going to get up and take a shower. I may die from being forced to get up too soon."

"Don't say that."

"All right, wise guy." Jackie pulled her son down for a reluctant kiss. "Then I'm going to take a shower, pick up all the broken glass, and then we'll go to the Tonington Tastee Treaterie and stuff ourselves like great white whales."

"Oh, boy!" Peter started to leave, then turned back, shy and confused. "Listen, you want another hug or something?"

"What the heck," Jackie responded.

By the time Jackie managed to shower and get dressed, the illusion show was over. Jackie carefully navigated her way down into the Reigerts' sunken living room and was startled to see her honor, Jane Bellamy, seated in a wheelchair. "Jackie!"

The damp-haired film instructor jumped. "Oh dear! Mayor Bellamy . . ."

"Jane," the mayor insisted, smiling evilly.

Jackie looked at the wheelchair with confusion. "What happened to you? If you don't mind me asking."

"Me? I thought you were the injured one. Oh, this . . ." Mayor Bellamy tapped her long red polished talons against the wheels of her chair. "This isn't real, silly. I mean it *is* real . . . Dick brought it from the hospital but . . ."

Jackie turned to see Richard Bellamy, M.D., a fifty-year-old neurologist with the sort of glowing, unlined skin that usually indicates a man is wearing makeup. He waved his briar pipe at her and Jackie couldn't help but notice that the bowl was in the shape of a skull.

" . . . I don't actually need a wheelchair," Jane Bellamy continued, waving her stiletto-heeled shoes around. "See."

"Uh, no."

"It's a party. You know I love to entertain at children's birthday parties . . ."

Jackie shuddered.

" . . . And of course dressing up as a clown as I do for my own . . ."—the ersatz invalid licked her lips as if hungry—

" . . . personal darling little children isn't appropriate for a twelve-year-old. Isn't that right, Peter?"

Jackie noticed her son giving the mayor a sickly smile and then sneaking out the patio door with Isaac.

"So, just to amuse your boy, I came as Joan Crawford in *Whatever Happened to Baby* . . ." The mayor tapped herself three times on the chest.

"Jane," Jackie said automatically.

"*Précisement*!" Jane agreed. "And of course no illusion—and that is the theme of this party, isn't it, illusions— of Joan Crawford would be complete without her Bette Davis counterpart. Bette!"

An elderly pasty-faced woman in a faded gingham frock turned with a big smile on her face.

"Jackie, you remember Merida Green, of course."

"Jacqueline," Merida greeted her with a big smile.

Jackie saw that the former department chairman had used dark wax to black out most of her teeth and nearly passed out again.

A growl from a familiar throat brought Jackie right back and caused Merida to withdraw her outstretched hand.

"Ha, ha!" Merida laughed, using barrels of air. "Of course your dog remembers me. What is its name?"

"Jake!" Jane Bellamy supplied, after consulting her ever-present note cards. The mayor of Palmer was not one to go to a public gathering of voters without knowing as much as she could about every person there.

"Of course," Merida slapped an unfiltered cigarette to her bee-stung lips and inhaled sharply. "Jackie and Jakey. So close. What I wouldn't give to have a powerful animal at my beck and . . ." Merida blew out a thin stream of smoke in a single breath. " . . . call."

Jackie fought the urge to flee and forced herself to say, "You know, Merida. President Foreman has asked me to help out with the investigation into the death of Walter Hopfelt."

"Dear Walter," the former prisoner smiled icily, waving her cigarette so that ashes flew everywhere. "I was shocked when I heard he was . . ."—Merida's voice dropped—" . . . *no more*."

"Only fifty-four years old," Jane Bellamy commented at once, reading from another card. "Still in the prime of his life. As old as you or I, Merida."

"Older," Merida hissed. "So, Jackie. You wish to talk to me?"

"Would that be convenient?" Jackie asked, forcing herself to keep her composure.

"Of course." As Merida smiled, the white pancake makeup on her cheeks cracked, revealing the pale, wrinkled skin below. "Isn't that adorable, Jane?"

"What's that, dear?" the mayor asked, pulling on her glasses.

"Darling Jacqueline wants to pick my brain on the criminal mind." Laughing hollowly, Merida picked up a shot glass of Cuervo Gold and threw it back. "Spend a few months out of a long life on 'Death Row' and all of a sudden you're an expert on murderers."

"You should be flattered, Merida," the mayor said. "You've become a veritable Anthony Hopkins."

"I prefer Susan Hayward, dear," Merida said.

"Of course you do." Jane stood up at once and turned to her husband. "Dick, will you show me again how to collapse this chair? I'm afraid I've quite forgotten."

While Dick Bellamy struggled to fold the heavy chair back up, the mayor of Palmer finished her husband's drink. It was a sloe gin fizz.

"We should go," she told Bill Reigert.

"Well, thanks for coming, Your Honor."

Jane fixed her eyes on Lil Reigert and gave her an appraising glance that made the young girl shiver. "You were wonderful, Lillien. I must take you in again."

Not wanting to encourage the mayor in any way, Lil just nodded.

"I'm finished, dear," Dick Bellamy announced. He had collapsed the wheelchair, but grease stains on his trousers and a bloody red handkerchief wrapped around a cut on his hand showed that the task had not been accomplished easily.

"Aren't you clever, dear?" Jane responded with a smile that didn't reach her eyes. "Merida."

"Jane."

"I'll leave you to your inquisitor."

"Thank you, Jane," Merida simpered. "As always."

Jane's eyes crinkled in sardonic amusement. "And your bird, dear?" Jane referred to a sickly gray and yellow canary which had been brought along in a gilded cage to act very simply as a prop.

"Oh, I'm sure I can get Tweeter home. Thank you. If not, then I'll just have to wring his skinny little neck." Merida shook the cage, and Tweeter cried in terror.

"You wouldn't really kill your little bird, would you?" asked the kind-hearted Lil. The twin magician hated the idea of animal abuse.

"Of course not," Merida assured the others in a husky, insincere voice. "I love birds. I've trained them since I was a short, chubby little girl."

"Come along, Dick," Jane called out as she strode for the door. "Jackie, do be more careful, dear. We'd hate to lose you. You're practically a Palmer institution."

Lil Reigert then melted away as well, and Jackie found herself alone with the paroled murderer.

"It's a pity, Jackie," Merida Green started, holding her

cigarette normally now, "that we've never been friends."

Jackie felt like saying, "A pity for whom?" but instead replied, "Yes, well, your trying to kill me put the kibosh on that one."

"Yes," Merida snarled in reply, "and your accusing me of murder didn't exactly warm my heart."

"But you did commit murder, Merida."

"Well, darling. There seems to be a difference of opinion on that one, so let's not quibble, shall we?" Merida picked up a corn trumpet and stabbed it, as if it were a stiletto, into the cream cheese dip. "It's as our former president used to say. Mistakes were made on both sides."

"Merida . . ." Jackie began.

"Yes, Jackie?" Merida sat down on a straight chair (one of two grouped around a chess table) and crossed her legs.

Jackie forced herself to look into her former co-worker's watery gray eyes. "You may have heard, as I was saying before, that the university has asked me to look into the death of Walter Hopfelt."

"Never met the man," Merida said at once.

"I find that hard to believe," Jackie stated, crossing her arms.

"If I really were a clever murderess, would I tell an easily disproved lie?"

"I don't know, not being a clever murderess myself."

Merida smiled thinly and lit a new cigarette from the butt of her old one. "Oh, you're too modest, Jackie. We have the death penalty in this state. I could have been electrocuted before the truth came out."

"Instead," Jackie pointed out, "you were paroled within a year and received a ten-thousand-dollar contract to write a book."

"Well, Jackie. Not that you've ever been fair before,

but why not try just this once in honor of your son's birthday . . . ?"

Jackie bristled. "If you ever go near my house or my family again . . ."

"Please, Jackie. Don't threaten me. It is against the law, you know." Merida smiled and toyed with the chess pieces (clowns, bareback riders, and ringmasters—all characters from the circus). "As I started to say, I spent over a year of my life in prison. Whether you think it was deserved or not, it was not pleasant. Prisons are noisy, you know, and I am very sensitive to sound. Prisons are very brightly lit, as well. They don't, for instance, turn off the lights when you go to bed, and I am also very sensitive to light. Worst of all, the guards are racists. That's an established fact. They are prejudiced against people like me and when you have a quarrel with a guard, they never believe the prisoner's side of it."

If Jackie felt any sympathy for Merida she hid it magnificently.

"As for the book," Merida continued, "if I were writing a tell-all about how I committed murder and escaped more serious punishment, I could understand your disapproval. But as you very well know, the book is about Lady Hitchcock. I had the makings of the deal in place before I went to prison. That's why the idea that I killed Philip because he cheated me out of a few hundred dollars is so laughable."

"Well, I hope you used your time away to do a lot of writing," Jackie commented.

"Now I know your notion of prison is taken from the movies. As I told you, I did not get on with the guards. They in turn denied me library privileges. Not that the prison's collection of out-of-date law books and condensed novels would have helped me. They gave me one sheet of paper a day. And a pencil. The guards were supposed to sharpen it. They didn't. I would claw my way to the lead with my fingernails." Merida held up her ugly scarred hands and nails so Jackie could see them.

"Well," Jackie responded, "you always did have strong fingers."

Merida let that one go. "I took a few notes in prison, Jackie. All told, less than a chapter's worth of material. I could have done as much in the Sabin Hughes Library in an afternoon." The former administrator then got to her feet. "What's the point in going on with this? You said you needed to ask me a few questions. I was perfectly willing to cooperate. Not because I'm some demented criminal genius with a special insight into every brain around me, but because I am honestly and truly a law-abiding citizen who wants to see all murderers in jail."

Merida didn't turn to see the skepticism on Jackie's face. She didn't have to. "Frankly, Jackie, despite the fact that I didn't kill him, I still believe the person who rid this world of Philip Barger didn't deserve to serve six months. I served almost three times that. Why not let it go?"

"I can't, Merida," Jackie said sharply. "Not when Danielle Sherman's death is still on the books as a suicide. Not when what happened to her may have had something to do with Walter Hopfelt's murder."

"Ridiculous."

"Want to put your money where your mouth is?"

"What?"

Jackie had Merida on the run and pressed her advantage. "Are you saying you didn't kill Danielle Sherman?"

"I am absolutely saying that."

"Then why not help me find out who did?"

This absolutely flabbergasted Merida. "You're mad!"

"More than likely," Jackie nodded. "I did have a blow

on the head, after all, but I'm serious about my proposition. I'm really in the dark on this one, Merida. The killing took place while I was out of town. The people involved won't talk to me. Not *really* talk to me. Anyway, you saw Jane Bellamy blow me off."

"And they'd talk to me?"

"In some cases. What are you afraid of?"

Merida met Jackie's look and smiled. A real smile this time. A dangerous smile. "Me? I'm not afraid, Jackie. I've looked death in the face a dozen times. What about you? Wouldn't you be afraid? To spend time alone—a lot of time—with the most dangerous woman in Palmer?"

"I'll have my bodyguard."

"Oh?"

Without being summoned, Jake came to his mistress's feet.

Merida smiled again, but warily moved back a step. "Well, in that case, then yes. I'd be happy to investigate murders with you, Jackie."

"Want to shake on it, partner?" Jackie asked.

Merida considered it, but realized that to shake hands she would have to move in closer to Jake. "No," she replied, slowly shaking her head. "That won't be necessary, Jackie. Your word alone is good enough for me."

CHAPTER 7

The first part of Jackie's evening was very enjoyable. Doing one more thing for Peter in honor of his birthday, Jackie invited over David Surtees, her colleague from the university. Peter had recently become interested in the Kennedy assassination, and David had given an interesting lecture on the subject (videotaped by Ral Perrin, the young cinematography TA at the university), which Jackie thought her son might enjoy.

"Cool!" was his response.

"What happened to 'excellent' ?" Jackie asked innocently.

"Mom," Peter said with what passed for affection these days, "you're such a gronk some times. Well, I gotta go to my party at Isaac's house. Mom, I mean Mrs. Cook is making my favorite type of cake."

"Strawberry shortcake?"

"That was Mike's favorite, Mom," Peter pointed out. "I like chocolate cake with coffee icing."

"You do?"

Peter shook his head, put his baseball cap on backward, and then left the house.

"Is he adopted?" David asked.

"I've just been kind of busy lately," Jackie mumbled. "So how have you been doing?"

"Okay," Surtees replied, splitting the last little bit of Madeira between their two glasses. "Finally over the Spanish Inquisition, or whatever I picked up in Barcelona. I'm just settling back to my usual routine now."

Jackie remembered that Surtees had spent most of the year before in Europe working as an editor on the Summer Olympics. "Are they ever going to do a videotape of the Olympics so those of us who never had time to sit down and watch it can catch up?"

"There'll probably be a dozen." Surtees chuckled. "You want to borrow some tapes? I've got a garage full of them."

"Well, maybe some time," Jackie mumbled.

"Are we perhaps a little too busy, Jackie?" the former Jesuit asked pointedly. "Do we maybe need to take some time to catch up with our family and our current events and let somebody else solve some of wicked Palmer's crimes?"

Jackie smiled, but didn't bite. "David . . ."

"What? Oh, no. Don't tell me this is about that videotape you wanted me to look at last spring under the infrared scanner. Talk about being busy. I still haven't gotten to it, I'm afraid. Do you still need it?"

"No. That's all right, David. Thank you." By now Jackie was used to the fact that half of the residents of Palmer never read the papers anymore and that as far as they knew or cared the murderer of millionaire industrialist Mannheim Goodwillie was still at large. "Are you finished?" she asked, pointing to the plates of beef stroganoff and chicken à la king that Peter had insisted on for his birthday dinner.

"Yes," Surtees replied, wiping his lips unnecessarily and tossing the cloth napkin on his plate. "An unusual combination. But thoroughly delicious."

"Good. There's a surprise strawberry shortcake for later, if you're interested."

Surtees laughed.

Jackie put away the dishes and came back with two brimming mugs of delicious Costa Rican coffee. "David, would you mind if I ask you something about a sensitive subject?"

"Uh-oh." He smiled mischievously.

"It's about Danielle."

"Oh." The young editing instructor's face adopted that haunted look that had become familiar since the death of his student girlfriend. Jackie thought of the pictures she had seen of Robert Kennedy at the funeral of his brother. Surtees had longer, darker hair than the former attorney general, and he parted it in the middle in the fashion once adopted by pop singers such as Jackson Browne. But otherwise he did resemble the brooding former senator from New York more than a little.

"I know this is painful for you," Jackie began.

Surtees's response was just a shrug. "We're born in pain, Jackie. We often die in pain. Sometimes the pain is good. It reminds us we're alive."

Jackie shivered. Jake immediately left his post under the dining room table and hopped up beside her on the couch.

"David, do you remember . . . ?"

Jake found a little burgundy meat sauce between two of Surtees fingers and obligingly licked them clean.

Surtees chuckled at the tickling. "Alex? Sure. How you doin' guy?"

Jake's ears picked up at once. It had been a long time since he had been called by a variation of his puppy name, "Alexander the Great."

"Where did you hear that name?" Jackie asked at

once, putting down her spoon.

"Isn't that him?" Surtees asked. "Isn't that what they called him when Matt Dugan owned him?"

"Yes . . . it is," Jackie responded, a little confused.

Surtees shrugged and sipped from his cup. "This is good coffee, by the way."

Jackie nodded. It was good coffee and she felt obligated to help the only country in the Americas that felt their tax-payers deserved to have programs that helped their people, not just a huge standing army. "You knew Matt Dugan?"

"Slightly," Surtees responded, taking a little pill out of a case in his pocket that helped him digest the lactose in the cream in his coffee. "When Danielle first came to the university. What was it, five years ago?"

Jackie nodded. Five years seemed about right. "Why did she know Matt Dugan?"

Surtees shrugged and added a little more brown sugar to his cup. "I think she was giving him information on things that were happening in her father's administration."

"Mayor Curtis," Jackie supplied.

"Big Bill," Surtees agreed. "That's why I was so relieved when they found out that Merida Green killed Danielle to keep her quiet about Phil Barger."

"Relieved?" Jackie asked.

"Yeah, in an odd sort of way. Otherwise, you know, I would have been convinced it had something to do with her father."

Jackie thought for a long moment, while Surtees sipped his coffee and stared placidly at the patterns the purple blobs were forming in her lava lamp.

"David . . ."

"Yes?"

"What if Merida Green didn't kill Danielle?"

Surtees almost choked on his coffee.

Jackie quickly leaned over and patted Surtees on the side of his neck (instead of, say, pounding on his back and making the problem worse). Then the doorbell rang.

Grabbing her cup of coffee—just in case she had to throw it in the face of an assailant—Jackie walked slowly to the door. Her loyal Alsatian was at her heels. "Who is it?" she called out.

"Xenia!" Jackie's duplex neighbor called out. "Can I come in for a moment, Jackie?"

Jackie sighed. Although she herself had never known Matthew Dugan, Jackie had felt sorry for his widow and children, who had come back to Palmer for the funeral. In a weak moment, she had suggested that perhaps Xenia and her two little girls would like to move into the empty apartment attached to her own. There hadn't been a day since that Jackie hadn't regretted her impetuous offer.

"Oh, you have company," Xenia protested as she sprung through the reluctantly opened door. "And look at me. I'm a mess!"

Xenia brushed back her thick black lustrous hair and ran her hands quickly down her body, clad in a tight aerobics outfit. Xenia Dugan, still in her early thirties (she had married at seventeen), was a short, splendidly curvaceous young woman with a beautiful low voice. Only a terrible, splotchy complexion that reacted negatively to almost every substance known to mankind kept Xenia from being a spectacular beauty.

"What can I do for you, Xenia?" Jackie asked. Forcing a smile, she knew her neighbor would probably have quite a list, as Jackie had been away all summer.

"Oh, where's little Peter?" Xenia asked.

"He's at his friend Isaac's house," Jackie answered.

"Oh, that's so horrible. You know, I knew I should have come down earlier but I had to hot oil my hair tonight and . . ." Having pulled tantalizingly at her hair for what Xenia obviously hoped to be just the right amount of time, she turned toward Surtees. "Who is *this*?"

Surtees, still a little strangled, slowly rose to his feet. "Hello, Mrs. Dugan," he greeted her.

"Oh . . ." Xenia danced coquettishly into the living room. "Do we know each other? You'll have to tell me who you are. I forgot my glasses upstairs and without them I'm simply—"

"Mrs. Magoo," Jackie provided. And this was not intended as a compliment. Unlike most television watchers, Jackie thought that Mr. Magoo was a spectacularly unfunny loon who should have been immediately retired to the senility wing of the Old Cartoon Characters Home.

"I'm David Surtees."

Xenia cut short her glare at Jackie to gush, "Oh, hi. It's so nice to meet you. My, aren't you handsome? Are you one of Jackie's *many* beaus?"

"No . . . I teach at the university with Jackie . . ."

Jackie gave Jake a pushing signal and then said loudly, "Well, Xenia. Thanks for coming down to welcome me back . . ." Of course Jackie knew full well that her neighbor had probably been eavesdropping at their shared bathroom wall.

"But, wait . . ." the tragic widow protested. It was all she could do as the former Mrs. Dugan got herded swiftly toward the door by the big German shepherd who artfully pulled first at one of Xenia's legs, then the other, nipping at the air around her knees whenever the young widow slowed for a moment. " . . . I wanted Peter to . . ."

"Actually, Xenia," Jackie responded, folding her arms. "I'm not really your landlord and Peter is not the building handyman. If you want some work done around the house, why don't you hire someone to do it? Goodnight now!"

Jake pushed Xenia out the door, closed it, and then twisted the deadbolt with his teeth.

"Kind of a pest, huh?" Surtees smiled.

"Had Irwin Allen lived, he could have done a disaster movie around her." Jackie sat down and gestured for Surtees to do the same. "I'm sorry to sound so harsh. Just take my word for it. Before I started taking a hard line, she was down here six or seven times a day, wanting favors, snooping on our lives, telling us endless stories of literally everything that had happened to her since her husband died . . ."

"Here, Jackie." Surtees poured her a little more of the highly caffeinated coffee. "Calm down."

"Sorry." Jackie laughed, throwing herself back in her chair. "She's . . . well, we should all try to be understanding of her. Maybe she's just been this way since her husband died. I don't know."

Surtees laughed and added a little vanilla sugar to his coffee. "I think, from what I remember Matt Dugan telling me, that she's been like that for some time."

Jackie shook her head, saddened to hear this prosaic reason for Matt Dugan's alcoholism. "David, did Danielle know Merida Green outside of school?"

"Not that I know of."

"Would she have met her at the old Blue Jay?"

Surtees shuddered. "No."

"You're sure?"

Surtees nodded. "Yes. I don't know why I never thought about this before. Trying to avoid the pain, I suppose."

Jackie started to tell him to forget the question, but Surtees shook his head.

"Dani never would have gone to a rough place like the Blue Jay with just a woman. Even if she trusted the woman—and Merida Green was not the most kindly, trustworthy soul."

"I know," Jackie said at once. "So you think whoever killed Danielle did it somewhere else and dumped her in the parking lot of the Blue Jay?"

"That sounds about right," Surtees responded, toying with his coffee spoon. "Which if true, puts Merida right back into it. Is it important to know whether Danielle really was there that night?"

"It might be," Jackie responded. "David, I think that the deaths of Danielle and Walter Hopfelt are connected somehow. Anything I can find out at this point about how Danielle died would be a help."

Surtees nodded, then took a pad out of his pocket. "Take this note to the night bartender, Milt."

Jackie looked up in some surprise. "Milt Gibson who used to work at the Juniper?"

Surtees nodded. "Now he and his wife work at the Blue Jay. Excuse me, Circus Maximus. Milt's my half-brother. When his dad died, my mother married his father. We all lived together for a little while. Milt's quite a bit older than me and he left home when I was eight years old, but he's always kept in touch. He has a remarkable memory for faces. He'd know whether Danielle had ever gone there or not."

"But if she was there more than once," Jackie asked, "would Milt remember whether she was there that particular night?"

"Rough as their reputation might be," Surtees responded dryly. "It wasn't every night that somebody dumped a body in their parking lot. Milt would remember."

Jackie got up and walked Surtees to the door. She gave him a little kiss on the cheek as they said goodnight.

"Have you dated anyone since Danielle died?"

"Are you asking me out?" Surtees joked.

Jackie laughed. "Seriously, David. Have you started to

think about other people? Not me, but sweet little things."

"Like your upstairs neighbor?"

Jackie made a face. "If that's what it takes. Listen, I know you can bury yourself in your work most of the time . . ."

"Can I ever."

"But that's not a solution," Jackie said firmly. "Take it from someone who's been there—sort of. When I got divorced, I had no intention of dating again for several years. Now, as my neighbor helpfully pointed out, I've dated a few men. And being with someone else—and I'm not just talking about sex—is very helpful sometimes. If you don't open yourself up to another person, eventually parts of you die."

CHAPTER 8

Circus Maximus in the daytime resembled nothing so much as a tool and die warehouse. The Circus's most effective bouncer, a gray, gnarled Korean named Kim Shan Nao, was repairing the chairs that had been damaged during the "killer" pigeon attack. Nearby was a baby carriage containing his granddaughter, Little Key, and next to him lay a toolbox filled with screws, silicate glue, and duct tape.

As Jackie watched, a large rat poked its head out from under the black plywood musician's bandstand. Jake immediately gave chase.

Milt Gibson, the tall, three-hundred-pound bartender with a red face, sandy gray hair, and an ugly brownish-red goatee, gave a snort of laughter and turned to Jackie. "That dog a mouser? You ever wanna give 'em away, lemme know. We got rats the size of chee-wow-wows around here."

Jackie, having already made one concession by wearing a tight, somewhat low-cut red and white polka dot dress, made a second one and pretended to chuckle at the big man's joke. "I think we'll probably keep him."

"Huh," Milt grunted. "What we? I thought you and Mac McGowan broke up."

Jackie gave the big bartender a smile that would have chilled ice.

Ignoring her clear message, Milt continued. "Too bad he dumped you. That captain's salary he's bringing home now ain't nothing to sneeze at." As if to illustrate the point, Milt then blew his nose lustily on the bar towel.

Jackie smiled again. Although Milt played the part of a lout to perfection, she remembered him from when he worked as day bartender at Reg White's tavern and knew that this crude act was probably a deliberate attempt to cut short her questioning. "*C'est la vie*, Milt. Oh, I'm sorry. That means, 'that's life.' Anyway, David thought you might be able to help me out a bit."

"I can see how that'd help you," Milt responded bluntly. "The part I don't get is how answering a bunch of police questions for someone who ain't a policeman is supposed to help me."

"Well"—Jackie dropped her smile completely now— "if you have any questions about my official status, you can talk to Chief Healy. It may even help you, Milt, to have a Palmer policeman pleasantly disposed to you. Especially when so many illegal things seem to keep happening here."

"Listen," Milt growled. "I got no problems with the police."

Jackie knew in a flash that this was true. Benjamin Horton, the new commissioner of the Palmer Police Department, a do-nothing career bureaucrat who had already been quietly removed from two other positions in city government, was not going to go after anyone.

"So what do you want to know?" asked the gruff bartender.

"Do you know this girl?" Jackie showed Milt a snapshot Surtees had given her.

Milt stared at the picture, then gave Jackie a droll look. "David's girly-girl."

"And an honor student at Rodgers U, where I teach."

"And a stiff who ended up in the old Blue Jay's parking lot with a set of works between her shapely little scoops."

"So you know quite a bit about Danielle Sherman," Jackie pointed out.

Milt then started cleaning his fingernails with the point of a can opener. "Just what I read in the papers, lady. You got any more questions? I wanna go in and sit down. I spend enough time on my feet as it is."

Suddenly, Jackie saw Jake trotting toward her with the rat in his teeth. Clearly the rodent had expired of a coronary, saving Jake the trouble of killing him. Jackie saw an opportunity to turn this to her advantage.

"My goodness. Look at that."

Milt nodded, disinterested.

"Let me see, Jake," Jackie urged, stifling a strong temptation to retch at the sight of the filthy animal. "Goodness. That's terrible. You know, Milt, you might not ever have any trouble from the police, but I don't think the Department of Health would let you keep your license if they knew you had vermin like this running around."

Milt gave Jackie a flat look, then yelled, "Becky!"

Rebecca Gibson, Milt's wife, came out of the kitchen, wiping her hands on the tails of the large shirt she was wearing. "What is it, Miltie?"

The waitress/cook of the Circus Maximus gave Jackie her usual unfriendly look. "What's she want?"

An overweight, brown-haired Betty Boop, Rebecca had been popular with the male customers at the Juniper Tavern until it was found out that she had, among other things, stolen change from their jacket pockets, and consistently overcharged unwary customers, doubling the sales tax or slipping by extra appetizers and drinks.

"Hi, Rebecca," Jackie said forthrightly. "Look what my dog found. The Circus isn't planning a 'Willard and Ben' night, is it?"

"Jeez," Rebecca exclaimed. "Look at the size of that sucker! Where'd you get it? The lady bring the rat in with her from the car, Milt?"

The big bartender started topping off the liquor bottles with tap water. "Either that or it ran in from the field. We don't get no mice in here."

"Course not," Rebecca unsurprisingly agreed. She then grabbed the rat by the tail and threw it across the room. "Kim!"

The elderly Korean turned and caught the flying rat neatly in his hands. Jackie winced.

"Dispose of that, will you?"

Jackie regarded the hard-boiled waitress, with her pudgy double chins and her bicep tattoo of a train entering a railroad tunnel, and decided on a new course of action. "Listen, Becky . . ."

The waitress turned, her nose in the air.

" . . . I'm not trying to give either of you a hard time. Really."

"No?" Rebecca asked. "Then you'll sign a waiver saying you ain't planning to sue us?"

"I'd be happy to," Jackie lied, leaning on the bar to ease the pain from her still painfully sore sacroiliac. "The university has asked me to ask some questions of some people that might help bring in the killer of Walter Hopfelt. You remember him? You used to call him when the Rodgers kids in here got rowdy."

"We've got nothing against Wally," Becky replied judiciously. "We're sorry to hear he passed on. But what's he got to do with that little tramp? Besides that she was a student at the university, I mean?"

Jackie gave Rebecca a sharp look, but gently bit her own lip before continuing matter of factly, "Well, I don't know what the connection was, Rebecca. Danielle wasn't a communications major and I didn't really know her all that well. You say she was very popular with the boys?"

"Well, I don't say popular and I definitely don't mean 'with the boys.' " Rebecca sniggered. "She liked to hang on 'men in uniform'—wouldn't you say, Milt?"

The big man guffawed and squirted the pretzels with an atomizer spray that concealed staleness.

Jackie shook her head slightly. This whole thing was getting very complex indeed. "Are you saying she liked policemen?"

"Blue Annies we call them," Rebecca explained, nodding. "Who'd she like? Let's see. Well, there was Max Dugan. What a hollow leg that guy had."

"Matt," Milt corrected.

"What?"

"Matt Dugan."

"What did I say?"

"Max Dugan. Like the movie on HBO."

"All right, Milt! Whatever." Rebecca turned to Jackie. "You see? That's why I call all the fellas 'Honey'—so gawd forbid I don't get one of the big babies' names wrong."

Jackie smiled in spite of herself. "Matt Dugan. The policeman? While he was still on the force?"

"Yeah," Rebecca answered, scratching her head with one finger. "Do I got dandruff, Milt?"

The big bartender yawned loudly.

"Okay, okay. Go sit in your chair. I'll finish here." As big Milt ambled off, Rebecca sat down on the end stool. "Honestly. You wonder how men find the energy to fight wars and stuff when whenever you ask them to do one little thing, they gotta spend the rest of the day in their lounge chairs resting up from it." The gum-cracking waitress reached behind the bar and brought up a bottle of Sprite. She drank a few swallows and then added a dollop of banana liqueur. "You want a drink or something? On the house, seeing you're almost a cop and all."

Jackie shook her head and tried not to wince as Becky smacked her lips over her drink. "Actually, Becky, I'm looking forward to getting out from under this amateur sleuth thing. I'd like nothing better than to have the police solve this case and go back to making up my lesson plans."

Becky reacted scornfully to the suggestion that the police could ever solve any crime. "C'mon, Jackie. The cops don't want to arrest anybody these days. They're all scared to lock anyone up for fear of being sued or that they'll have to turn the football stadium into a jail to house all the people who have been getting away with things for years because they know the cops don't give a damn. Can you imagine Palmer Stadium just filled to the goalposts with people in handcuffs? And how appropriate would that be with half the Palmer football team charged with sex crimes? What are they, the Palmer . . . ?"

"Pythons," Jackie supplied. And needless to say the avid fans were always calling Frances and Bara Day to borrow their pets as mascots during the tailgate parties.

"The Trouser Snakes, they should be calling them . . ."

Jackie made a face. Hoping to get Rebecca back on track before she drank any more, she resumed speaking. "You were saying you saw Danielle here with Matt Dugan, when he was on the force. That must have been six or seven years ago. She would have been fifteen, sixteen."

Rebecca shrugged. "You can't keep the tall ones out, Jackie. They've all got fake ID's and if you challenge them their parents turn around and sue you."

Jackie shook her head, thinking fleetingly of Peter. She had been clenching her teeth so often lately she was gettng migraine headaches. "You don't really think she was dating Matt, do you, Rebecca?"

Rebecca saw the attentive Jake giving her a look and started. "Why he's looking at me like that? He hungry? We got some Spicy Pete sticks here somewhere if he wants them."

"No, he's just . . ."

Rebecca kept eyeing the big German shepherd with apprehension. "What? I didn't do nothing to him. He some sort of doggie lie detector, or something?"

"I think he's reacting to us talking about Matt," Jackie explained. "They were partners, you know."

Rebecca immediately reacted to the intellectual challenge. "Sure, I knew that. After Wally quit the force to take the job at the U, Matt switched over to the Canine Corps. They had him on bow and arrow restrictions, you know?"

Jackie recognized the term used by policemen for other men in blue who had been controlled-substance compromised and were therefore restricted from carrying a loaded weapon or driving a police vehicle. She hadn't known that Matt Dugan had gotten to that stage while still on the force—unless of course it was all part of an elaborate undercover charade.

"Then he worked with Connie Mitchell," Becky Gibson resumed. "Then it was just him and the dog. Then he got fired for taking a poke at the mayor."

"Matt Dugan punched Mayor Curtis?"

"Sure. Right over there." Rebecca pointed to a murky corner with her drink straw. "It's lucky it was late and there weren't so many people around to recognize them. Talk about hushing things up. We tiptoed around here with ball gags in our mouths for weeks."

Jackie shook her head in amazement. "I didn't hear anything about that."

Rebecca snorted. "Well, you wouldn't, would you? Not when the *Chronicle* and the *Gazette* and the other newspapers were all owned by Big Bill's millionaire drinking buddies. You gotta have it spelled out for you, honey?"

Jackie flinched as Rebecca's hand came down on her arm.

"That little tramp Danielle was spying on her father," Rebecca resumed. "She tipped off Matt Dugan. He'd been looking to get something on someone in City Hall forever."

Jackie's brain flash-danced with connections. In the months of putting up with Xenia Dugan, Jackie had been told many times of Matt's honest Republican alderman father, Matthew Senior, who had served capably in the administration of Palmer's finest mayor ever, the conservative great communicator, His Honor, Ward Clement. Matt Senior had married Clement's sister and then, as the new commissioner of police, had been the one to redesign the Palmer Police Department along the lines of New York police stations (including the unusual choice to call the station houses by the idiosyncratic New Amsterdam word "precinct"). Apparently when the Curtis machine had gotten in after Clement's sudden death, Dugan had been quickly hounded out of office, and shortly thereafter out of politics altogether, on trumped-up charges.

"She talked to Dugan and his partners," Rebecca prated on, "maybe about bad stuff that was really going down or maybe only Matt was stupid enough to try to make something out of it . . ."

"Big Bill Curtis did leave City Hall under a cloud," Jackie pointed out.

"Only 'cause they were so sloppy in killing Mattie,"
Rebecca responded. "He would have been dead in a couple
of months anyway the way he was falling apart. But they
couldn't wait, so they killed him." Rebecca tried and failed
to stifle a belch. "That shut up Danielle and the others.
Then when the heat was off, they knocked off the others,
one by one. Danielle, Wally . . . heck, Con Mitchell better
be careful. He's the only one of that old gang left."

CHAPTER 9

As Jackie's Jeep sped toward its next destination, red flashes of lightning lit the sky and thin white wispy clouds passed over the moon, making it look like some cosmic barber pole.

"Strange weather," Jackie commented.

Jake, beside Jackie on the passenger seat, raised one eyebrow.

"I don't know, big fella . . ." Whenever Jackie was nervous she talked to Jake. He may not have understood all of what she told him, but he was a damn good listener. "Merida Green is free. No one thinks that it's unusual but me. No one thinks she's dangerous anymore. I mean, wherever she goes, she's treated like royalty. No wonder Jane Bellamy is her best buddy all of a sudden. If Merida Green were to run for mayor against her, she'd probably win."

The moon was gone now. The clouds had swelled to mattresses and, like waterbeds, they opened, sending torrents of rain straight down. Jackie flipped on her wipers and started to roll up her window.

"Jake."

The big dog leaned over, took the knob in his teeth, and started to roll up his window as well.

Jackie brushed some excess moisture off Jake's noble brow with a paper napkin. "I don't know, partner. Nobody believes that Merida Green killed Danielle Sherman. Half the people think she didn't kill Philip Barger. And I know I can't be this far wrong. I'll tell you one thing though, Jake. If I am wrong about this, I'll never agree to act as an amateur detective again."

Lightning again ripped the sky.

It made Maury in the backseat whimper.

Jake dropped his head and slowly shook it back and forth in disgust.

Jackie then turned back to her new dog, Jake's year-old son, and said in a firm voice, "Maury, shut up!"

It had definitely not been Jackie's idea to get this second dog. Maury had forced himself on her.

Jackie cast her mind back to earlier in the day, after she had rushed back from her side trip to the Circus Maximus to do her four o'clock film lab. Jackie was already ashamed of herself for missing so many classes in the last year because of her sleuthing. She felt even worse when a gangly young black student, Khalil Moore, chatting intimately with Lynn Fevre, the Communications Department's prize student (it was the young girl's ambition to become a tap-dancing weatherperson), was so startled by Jackie's entrance he cried out, "Who are you?"

Deeply embarrassed, Jackie had relieved her teaching assistant, Arne Hyverson (a chunky, blond Norwegian-American who had worked extensively as a writer of action films during the period when Canada had offered generous tax breaks to lousy filmmakers), and then spent some time telling the students about her adventures working on the *CopLady* telefilm. She had just finished showing a blooper reel (inevitable in these days when no less than four weekly programs were devoted to bloopers, flubs, practical jokes, and carefully staged and rehearsed amateur "Candid Camera"–type videos), when all of a sudden the door flew open and Fred Jackson, assistant chairman of the department, burst in carrying the biggest puppy Jackie had ever seen.

"Ho, ho, ho," cried the burly cinematography instructor. "Not that I'm old Kris Kringle. Or even Edmund Gwenn. I mean, I do have a beard. But it isn't white. Now Chairman Quest has white hair, but he isn't even here—thanks to your pretty instructor over there."

This remark had made Jackie feel a little guilty. She had heard that Ivor Quest, after all his exertions (physical and emotional), had been forced to take off some time to regroup.

"I don't know where Chairman Quest is," Fred continued. "Maybe the North Pole. Ho, ho, ho. But I don't think so."

The students all gave Fred a blank look. Acting Chairman Jackson was a capable instructor, well liked by the students, but he was easily the least funny man in Palmer.

Fred Jackson then turned to the students and said, "So, kids. Did you miss your instructress these past few weeks while she's been away on a special assignment?"

"Not really," Khalil the rat had immediately responded, obviously wanting to get even with Jackie for startling him. "We've been seeing a lot of movies with Cyril Plum. He's really terrific."

The young student referred to the most recent addition to the communications studies faculty. Cyril Plum had come over after being mandatorily retired from Rodgers's local academic rival, Assissi of Palmer.

One of the last of the great pulp writers, Plum had taken refuge in academia, fleeing from a world which wanted no more of his *Joshua, Lord of the Jungle*. Of course the moment he buckled down to being a great writing teacher, the offers started pouring in for radio, motion picture serial, early television series, and later, cable tel-

evision rights for *Joshua*. Early in his career Plum had taken
personal leave from Assissi to enthusiastically plunge into
each new manifestation of his great series. Finally, having been beaten to the consistency of warm manioc (the
preferred dish of the vegetarian Joshua), Plum had left
the development of his literary children to less capable
hands and instead buried himself in teaching and endlessly
viewing the great Hollywood movies of his youth.

"Oh, you like Professor Cyril, do you?" Fred boomed
happily. It had been his idea to recruit the old writer of
vine-swinging tales.

Lynn Fevre, foolishly assuming that none of the faculty
were competitive or jealous of each other, chimed in with,
"Yeah, we just saw *Suspicion*. And last week we saw
Rebecca. So it's like Mr. Plum really knowledged us out
on 'em."

"Man is really conversant with his Hitchcock," Khalil
added, again intent on heckling Jackie (who had earlier
made some innocuous slip of the tongue while discussing a minor Hitchcock/Henry Fonda thriller called *The
Wrong Man*).

"Glad to hear it!" Fred yodeled. It was clear to all of
them that he hadn't really been interested in the answer, but
obviously he felt that in his new role as acting chairman he
had a certain obligation to pretend to have a dialogue with
the students. "Anyway, Jackie. This belongs to you."

Jackie looked down at the large animal Fred Jackson
had put down on the floor in front of her and asked,
"How so?"

"It was shipped to you," Jackson said. "From Los
Angeles."

Jackie's feverish mind immediately turned to Ronald
Dunn and how she could most painfully kill him for sending
her this insane, preposterous gift.

"From the Los Angeles police, in fact," Fred elaborated. "This guy a clue or something?"

"No," Jackie had replied in horror, immediately making the connection. "This is Jake's son."

"Oh," Fred replied dubiously. "Then congratulations, Jackie. You must be very happy."

Fred and some of the students politely applauded or clapped her on the back. One student offered Jackie a cigar, which she declined. They acted as if she had become a grandmother or something. Jackie looked down at her new acquisition. It was the largest puppy anyone had ever seen. A veritable Shetland pony. As Jackie stared at the surprise gift, she realized she would probably keep the pup, but wondered just the same what the proper etiquette was when your dog impregnated someone else's dog. Should you kick in for a gift? Should you offer to share medical expenses? If they offered one or more puppies to you, were you morally obligated to take them? To find them a new home if you did not want them yourself?

While all of these thoughts raced up and down the ladders of her mind like so many Super Mario brothers, Maury, the giant mastiff/Alsatian puppy, came over and licked her hand. She had looked down at the big puppy's tongue. It was like being rubbed down by a wet towel. Seeing that this pleased his mistress, Maury obligingly did it again. Unfortunately, this time the smell of Jackie's hand lotion bothered him and he sneezed lustily.

"Ooogh-uhhh!" Fred had then exclaimed in disgust. "That's repulsive! Don't just stand there, students. Get your instructor some towels."

From that point on, things went from bad to worse. Jackie quickly found out that her new best friend was as noisy and as undisciplined as Jake was obedient and quiet.

During the lab, Maury had two accidents, managed to bark loudly whenever the video viewer came on, and at one point knocked Khalil Moore off his chair when the poor student's wristwatch alarm had gone off.

In the hall corridor after class, Maury shouldered a fire extinguisher off its hook, causing it to go off, making a mess of Jackie's shoes and most of the surrounding corridor.

Later still, in Jackie's cubicle, Maury had managed to wrap himself in two-thirds of Jackie's computer pinfeed continuous-roll paper and finally, in the Jeep on the ride home, the mastiff puppy scratched the expensive back seat upholstery to shreds.

At home, the big puppy had licked the television set, giving himself a shock that made him cry out loud, blood-curdling howls. Then, seeing Peter practicing with his hockey stick on the kitchen floor (something his mother had asked him a dozen times not to do), Maury had hip checked the young athlete out through the open backdoor and onto the lawn.

Peter, finding himself sprawled out on a relatively comfortable surface, had decided to turn the occasion into a special nap session.

Jackie hadn't known this, of course. When she came home from shopping and saw Maury with dripping red fangs (from chomping on all the tomatoes in Jackie's garden) and her son prone and lifeless, Jackie nearly had a coronary.

Now, with Jake along as a babysitter, Jackie was motoring to the Police Dog Academy, formerly the Palmer Canine Academy, and before that the Sweeten Dog Academy.

"What a day!" Jackie said aloud. As she did, they passed the sign for the Police Dog Academy, bearing a cartoon likeness of Cornelius Mitchell, Jake's old instructor. He lived there now, taking care of all the abandoned dogs the former owner Tom Mann (now deceased) had collected in his lifetime. He also cared for a number of strays and wild dogs which, now that the city dog pound had been closed by court order, the Canine Rights Lobby had insisted that the City of Palmer house in lavish comfort.

Jackie didn't like this place at all. Jake, beside her, clearly felt the same way. She could tell from his thoughtful look that he was remembering in his own black-and-white way the day they had chased a murderer through the building.

Jackie gave her loyal associate a brief hug and he snapped back to the present with an embarrassed woof.

Crawling along now, finding it very difficult to see the road in the rain and mist, Jackie wondered why she felt a strange sense of foreboding.

Was it the buildings of the Academy itself? No—they were actually rather handsome. It wasn't like the Barger house, for instance, on Faculty Row. Ever since that particular house's owner had died, strange sounds and sights—odd crashing noises and ghostly lights—had been heard and seen. Fred Jackson had told Jackie he'd thought of buying the place, but scotched the idea when, while taking a tour of the house, someone or something had made it impossible for him to keep his pipe lit.

No, this was different. The Police Dog Academy just had too many unpleasant memories. All of a sudden, Jackie thought she saw something above her. She heard a ghostly scream and then thought she saw someone hurtle down off the roof and crash onto the cobblestones below.

Jackie's nightmarish vision was disturbed by another howl. This one was more plaintive than ghostly. Jackie looked down and saw Maury with his head stuck between the two seats and laughed aloud. "You are nothing but trouble, aren't you?"

Maury panted happily and with his nose nudged the Jeep's gear shift into reverse.

The Jeep immediately lurched backward off the road and into the surrounding swampy muck. Jackie and Jake were thrown back in their seats, then into darkness as the car stalled and the generic "Die-Easy" battery Michael McGowan had installed for Jackie as a birthday surprise expired. Mistress and dog turned to glare at Maury. Fortunately they had been wearing both their belts and their shoulder harnesses and so were uninjured.

"What have you done, you crazy dog?" Jackie exclaimed, as she recovered her wits.

Maury chuckled, amused by his own faux pas, and inserted his head under Jackie's hand, urging her to pat him. Jackie mistressed the urge to vigorously massage Maury's thick cranium with the heavy flashlight she kept bracketed under the seat, and instead opened her door to see just how badly they were mired in the mud.

Pretty bad.

She got out of the Jeep, with Maury jumping out behind her, and shook her head. Unfortunately, the head shaking gave the already muddy Maury the notion to imitate his new owner.

"Oh, man!" Jackie cried as her new puppy shook dog-smelling water over her. She was now thoroughly soaked. Stifling an impulse to kick her new ward, Jackie then looked at the soft spot her left rear tire was stuck in.

"All right," she said to herself aloud (hoping against hope the sound of a human voice would keep zombies at bay). "This isn't too bad, but I can't do it myself." Jackie stepped back and prepared to marshal her four-legged troops. "Maury, I'll need your muscle power. Jake!"

Jackie called out. Her loyal companion at once daintily tiptoed to her side. "I'll need your brains. Go get a rock to put behind the tire so it doesn't slide back on us while we're pushing. Don't get anything too blocky. I want more of a smooth oval over . . . oh, you know what I mean."

Jake nodded intelligently and disappeared into the night rain.

Jackie turned to the merry Maury, now digging a hole in the mud. "Maury . . ."

Maury was distracted from replying by the sight of the wet goopy mud sliding in to fill the hole he had just dug. Wiping his snout with both of his big front paws, Maury redug the hole and watched befuddled as the same thing happened again.

"Maury!" Jackie yelled, grabbing the enormous flea collar that the state of California required dog owners to put on their pets before traveling to another state. "I want you to push the Jeep. Do you understand?"

Maury gave a look, then turned back to Jackie as if asking, "Could you repeat the question?"

"Push, push." Jackie demonstrated by putting her shoulder to the back of the Jeep (getting herself wetter than ever) and giving it a good shove.

Maury responded by looking up at the sky, as a big drop of water hit his nose, as if to say, "Hey, who did that?"

"Push!"

Finally getting the idea, the big puppy swung into action.

Just then Jake came back with a perfectly shaped river rock. The intelligent police dog took in the situation and immediately brought the stone over and put it in Jackie's hand. Distracted by a rabbit somewhere in the distance, Maury turned his head. Jackie hefted the stone, feeling the weight of it in her hand. Jake nodded, once, twice, three times as if to say, "Do it. Just do it!"

Jackie found herself actually saying aloud, "Who would ever know?"

Just then, a man crashed through the woods toward them. Jake countered protectively in front of Jackie and then the wet-haired film instructor recognized Cornelius Mitchell.

"Well," the thin, sour-faced man in black heavy-weather gear snarled at them. "Now that you're finally here you might as well come inside."

The Academy had undergone another drastic interior renovation since Jackie had last been there. Originally the building had been the headmaster's residence in a boys' academy. As such it had been vaguely military looking, with nothing fragile around that a clumsy adolescent boy could break.

When the Academy was lost to unpaid back taxes, Mel Sweeten bought the buildings, sold the old boys' academy to a landfill company, and remodeled the rest. The headmaster's residence became Sweeten's home and Mel Sweeten, something of a loon in his last years, had driven his wife as crazy as himself by buying dozens of arcane products all with pictures of, or cut in the shape of, beagles. The effect was bizarre, and reminded those who visited the Sweetens of the set of a cheap South American soap opera.

In any case, the grounds of the boys' academy were turned into kennels and dog runs, and the old boys' dorm became a storage facility with indoor training and grooming rooms for show dogs. Another part of the old boys' dorm became a small apartment for a live-in trainer. That residence had been occupied for a time by Tom Mann, the third owner.

When Tom Mann took over the Academy he invested what little money he had in paying the back taxes all over again (a slick trick the city got away with by assuming that

Mann would not know what Sweeten had already coughed up). After the punishing town levy, the former dog trainer did not have much money left to refurbish the building. He therefore cut off most of the areas he didn't need and furnished the rest with various pieces salvaged from his second-hand stores (including a fairly valuable set of Golden Age Radio memorabilia).

The current look, undertaken by the present owner, Con Mitchell, was rustic Americana—and before Jackie could snap out of her reverie, Maury had attacked (and quickly broken to pieces) a scarecrow in the entrance hall.

"Maury!" Jackie yelled. The puppy immediately brought over the painted coconut-shell head and set it near the feet of his beloved mistress for her inspection and approval.

Jackie turned to Con Mitchell. "I'm terribly sorry."

"That's all right," the pinched-faced, tightly muscled police sergeant replied. "I'm sure if I go to enough expensive galleries I'll eventually find another one-of-a-kind priceless antique like that one."

"I really do feel terrible," Jackie repeated.

"Stuff happens," Mitchell snarled. "Problem is, I got a lot of 'fragibles.' Are we going to lock this goofy mutt up?"

"No!" Jackie retorted indignantly. "How can you of all people say that?"

"What?" Mitchell asked as he placed the remnants of the museum piece in a special straw recyclables bin. "They've revoked freedom of speech for cops now?"

"Con." Jackie struggled to retain her temper. "You work with dogs . . ."

Mitchell gave her a disgusted look. "Yeah, I work with paper clips too. I don't have any particular fondness for them either."

Jackie backed off a step from the dog handler.

"Not everyone," Mitchell continued, "who handles dogs does it out of sheer love for their canine counterparts. You want to see how I like dogs?"

Con led Jackie into the first interior room, once a formal dining room, now a gloomy display hall of some kind. The police dog trainer then flipped a switch, turning the track lights on. "Welcome to the Canine Chamber of Horrors!"

Jackie flinched as she saw Diablo, a Great Dane once owned by Tom Mann, and the fat, stupid Raphael, a mutt that Mel Sweeten had once tried to sell as the offspring of his two champion beagles. Both dogs had been stuffed and made to act as the centerpiece of dramatic dioramas.

"Oh, my gosh," Jackie exclaimed.

Mitchell giggled fiendishly. "Every police department has its Black Museum. This is going to be Palmer's. Like it?"

It nearly took Jackie's breath away. "It's the most macabre thing I've ever seen in my life."

"Thank you." Con Mitchell smirked. "Big pooch and little pooch were tenants of the property before I bought this place. I agreed to take care of them and they unfortunately passed on shortly thereafter. Taxidermy's a very therapeutic hobby. You should try it some time. Jake's not going to live forever, you know."

With much effort, Jackie restrained herself from slapping Mitchell's face.

"Hee, hee, hee," weaseled the Palmer central precinct dog handler. "What are you so nervous about?"

Jackie backed off, averting her eyes from the garish diorama displays at the end of the room. "To be honest," Jackie replied, somewhat disingenuously, "it's this place. The last two times I was here I had a long scary conversation with a murderer. At least I don't have to face that tonight."

"Don't be so sure," Con responded quickly. "Jackie, you know my lady love Merida, don't you?"

Jackie's head shot around and a grim smiling figure in a long black dress, her hair pulled back in a severe bun, greeted her. "Here you are. Welcome partner."

Jackie forced a smile.

"What did I tell you, Con?" Merida said, linking arms with her beau. "I knew if we waited long enough, sooner or later she would come to us."

CHAPTER 10

Jackie didn't get molested at the Academy. The conversation had been fairly bizarre, however. The tone had been distinctly chilly, but protected by her two dogs, Jackie had gotten out of the house without any untoward moves toward her.

Jackie had also managed to get her battery jumped with the help of Michael McGowan, and had been given a warm blanket to wrap around her chilled shoulders as she drank a big warm mug of fresh-roasted coffee. *The hard part, the really hard part*, Jackie thought to herself as she snuggled in her favorite seat in her old boyfriend's apartment, *was facing him and saying*, "I really appreciate your help, Mike."

"We're here to serve." McGowan smiled a little sadly. "How have you been, Jackie?"

Jackie smiled, just as sadly. Part of her, she knew, still loved Michael McGowan. "I'm fine. You know, I've been away most of the summer."

"So I heard," the friendly policeman said. "Working on a TV show."

"Well"—Jackie played with a strand of her hair—"it was was really more of a TV movie."

"Oh, no," McGowan replied, not actually, in fact, all that concerned. "Did I just make some terrible, hick Midwest faux pas?"

"No." Jackie smiled. "But that's why Hollywood types call everything 'projects.'"

"I sit corrected."

Jackie looked out the living room window, mostly to see if anyone was hanging around on the ledge looking in. It was an unreasonable fear, but Jackie hadn't been over to McGowan's apartment for a while, and so felt a little apprehensive. "And what is all this stuff about being a barefoot boy from the Midwest? I happen to know you're from Rhode Island."

"Ah, you remember." McGowan smiled. "You're quite a detective. Even without your dog."

"I hope to goodness they're not wrecking your laundry room," Jackie said, worried.

McGowan chuckled. "If they cause enough damage to make the building management replace those old washer-driers, all us tenants will be very happy."

"So—how does it feel being a captain, Michael McGowan?"

The policeman actually sighed. "It's . . . it's pretty dull, actually. Lots of meetings, lots of inspections, lots of paperwork and pretending to look interested or concerned while citizens and politicians rail at you. If it weren't for the pay raise, Jackie, I wouldn't have taken it."

"Oh." Jackie felt a little sad. "That's too bad."

McGowan's face broke into a sad Irish smile. "Don't get me wrong, though. It isn't any hardship. It's just not what I expected."

Jackie nodded and then cautiously changed the subject. "Can I ask you for some advice?"

McGowan's eyes crinkled with amusement. "For your project?"

"No, for Walter Hopfelt." Jackie saw a troubled look come over the police captain's face and quickly explained.

"The U wants me to poke my nose into another investigation."

"Poor you," McGowan replied with a hint of sarcasm.

Jackie let it roll off her now dry back. "I'd rather be a captain, frankly. What can you tell me about this one, Michael?"

Still a little annoyed, the homicide captain threw up his hands. "Hey, I'm just a professional policeman. What would I know about crime?"

Jackie's eyes squeezed partially closed in amusement. "Well, not much obviously, compared to a frizzy-haired film instructor and her amazing police dog . . ."

" . . . K-9 . . ." McGowan corrected.

" . . . Jake," Jackie continued. "But I'm hoping you'll say something in your own bumbling fashion that will somehow give me the key that solves the crime."

"Like Doctor Watson," McGowan responded dryly.

"Precisely!"

The former couple shared a laugh and then McGowan said, "All right, then. I'll do anything to keep you from resorting to the needle . . ."

Jackie returned with, "Home-baked cookies, actually, used to be my main vice."

"And good cookies they were."

"All right, out of the grocery freezer," Jackie confessed. "While other girls were learning to cook, my father had me watching Nunnally Johnson films for structure."

"He wrote the script for *The Grapes of Wrath*, didn't he?"

Jackie was impressed. "Very good. You've been reading your textbooks."

"The world is so horrible to most policemen, Jackie," McGowan explained, "that sometimes we unplug all the phones and sit around the war room watching old movies."

"I've suspected as much," Jackie joked back. "Are donuts consumed?"

"It's been known to happen."

The couple shared another laugh and then Jackie asked, "Tell me about Hopfelt. He was on the force at one time, wasn't he?"

McGowan nodded. "Briefly. Well, actually I guess it was a few years, but only briefly while I was on the force. Walter was over on the civil side. More or less a bench jockey. Like me now."

There was a moment while McGowan contemplated that newly considered truth. Jackie let him have the time alone and took the opportunity to admire her favorite McGowan furnishing, a glass lamp which had a long thin base filled with water. A motor in the lamp tilted the water back and forth like a teeter-totter, and a looping tape contributed the sound of the ocean. The effect was very restful.

"Anyway," McGowan resumed, "most of his job was paperwork, but they'd occasionally send him out on civil actions."

"Foreclosures?" Jackie asked.

McGowan nodded again. "Foreclosures, forced sales, evictions . . ."

"Aren't those nice city marshals in charge of that?" Jackie asked.

"Yes," McGowan answered his former girlfriend. "But this being Mellencamp country and all, we tend to send an armed policeman along so the evictees don't start shooting."

Jackie shook her head. Like so many Midwesterners, she was appalled at the number of homeowners and small-spread farmers who were being turned out of their residences after the looting and closings of the local savings and loans.

"I've got to ask then," Jackie inquired, "if there's any possibility that a disgruntled former homeowner killed him?"

"It's possible," McGowan responded dubiously. "Worth having Healy check through Hopfelt's stuff. Problem is, that was a long time ago—and before the recent rash of evictions. I would think the present guys would be more in danger. Hopfelt lost his city deputy job almost six years ago—when the city went civil service, he couldn't pass the test."

"That's funny," Jackie commented. "He seemed like a pretty smart guy."

"He was," McGowan responded. "But lots of smart guys don't test well. I was a wreck before the captain's test—and I didn't pass by a lot, believe me."

Jackie smiled sympathetically.

McGowan bit his lip, then continued, "Anyway, after Hopfelt lost his post downtown, the department offered him his old job back on the west side. As a uniformed police officer. It wasn't a great offer, but they didn't even have to do that much. By law."

Jackie reached out her hand and put it on the back of McGowan's. "He must have felt it was quite a comedown."

"Yeah," the captain responded. "And felt it in spades. Especially when his partner was a bow and arrow squadder."

"Matt Dugan?" Jackie guessed at once.

McGowan nodded again. "And it's possible, Jackie—not definite, just possible—that maybe these two guys, embarrassed and desperate as they were to put themselves back on a better standing, stretched a point or two. Maybe they didn't even do anything wrong. They just listened to Danielle Sherman. And maybe Danielle Sherman knew something."

"And maybe she didn't," Jackie pointed out.

McGowan nodded. "Either way, it got her killed."

They listened to the waves from the wave machine for a moment. Then Jackie asked, "Con Mitchell—how does he fit into this?"

McGowan was a little startled by the transition. "Does he?"

"The bartender at the Circus Maximus . . ." Jackie explained, " . . . the old Blue Jay, says he was there, talking to Danielle Sherman the night she was murdered. The bartender's wife says that she and other witnesses can confirm it."

McGowan leaned back in his chair, took a puff from his corncob pipe, and considered. "Well, I suppose it could have been a lot of things. Do we rule out the social? Con was thought to be something of a ladies' man at one time."

Jackie considered saying, "More than you?" but bit her lip.

McGowan saw the impulse in her eye and finally said what he had started to say several times. "I'm sorry you walked in on me and Sylvia."

Jackie started as if hit in the stomach.

"I don't know why I did that. Why I gave you a key, then still dated, still slept with other women." McGowan took a deep breath. "I know I didn't do it to hurt you."

"It did hurt me," Jackie said softly. In fact, Jackie hadn't talked to her friend Marcella in months, not because she was mad at her, but because the local station newswoman had been with her that night and the memories were still too painful.

"I know. It hurt me too," McGowan said softly. "Really. I feel things for you, Jackie, that I've never felt for anyone. I don't know that that's a good thing."

Jackie smiled noncommittally.

McGowan's pain-filled blue eyes met hers head-on. "Obviously I wasn't ready for a serious commitment so soon after my divorce. I don't think . . . I know I'm not ready for a commitment now. I don't know if you're seeing someone else . . . I haven't asked."

"It's a small town, Michael," Jackie replied in a soft voice. "You wouldn't have to ask. Any number of people would be glad to tell you. Even if you weren't a policeman."

"Touché," McGowan responded. "I deserved that. All right, Jackie. I know you're dating someone. And I'm still dating Sylvia. I don't know how serious any of us are about each other. And tonight, frankly, I don't care. All I know is I want you to spend the night here with me, and I'll say anything or do anything in the world to make that happen. I'm asking. What do you say?"

Before Jackie could answer, there was a loud knock on the door. McGowan opened it and saw two of his detectives, John "Jack" Mason and "Buck" Bendix standing on his doorstep. Both men were big, square-jawed, and square-shouldered former football tackles with closely cropped hair and well-polished, square-toed shoes. Jack Mason, resembling Robert Stack (in his Elliot Ness years), did the talking.

"Captain McGowan."

"Yes. What is it, John?" McGowan hated to use nicknames.

"Sorry to bother you, sir, but we need you to come with us."

McGowan's face clouded over with consternation. "For what?"

Never one to beat around the bush, Mason answered in his flat Midwestern voice, "There's been a murder, sir."

McGowan was completely unimpressed by this piece of news. "We get a hundred and twenty murders a year, Mason. This couldn't wait 'til morning?"

The big policeman slowly shook his large head. "No, sir. There's been a killing, sir. In Robin Hill."

"Robin Hill!" McGowan raged. "That's not even our district."

"No, sir," Detective Mason agreed. "But the deceased is an officer, sir. Sergeant Mitchell."

"Con Mitchell?"

"Yes, sir." Mason consulted a notebook as he talked. "Someone tossed a homemade hand grenade into his house, where he was staying. Killed him outright. Put his lady friend in the hospital. Chief Healy sent us to get you, sir. He requested you personally."

McGowan swallowed hard, then pivoted on his heel. "I'll get my coat."

Jackie stared out at the two men still visible through the open door. "Excuse me . . . Detective?"

"Detective Sergeant Jack Mason, ma'am," the detective replied, putting his notebook back in his jacket pocket.

"Do you know who I am?"

"Yes, ma'am. Ms. Walsh."

"May I ask you a question?"

Mason gave his partner Bendix a consulting look. The silent detective nodded and shrugged a "What the heck?"

"The woman that was with Con Mitchell. Was it by chance, Merida Green?"

Mason gave Jackie a long look, then nodded. "You know anything that might help us with this, Ms. Walsh?"

"Maybe."

Bendix immediately took out his notebook. He opened to the last page of it and immediately saw something that made him start. "Hey, Jack!"

Mason turned and looked at the entry his partner was pointing to. He then turned slowly to Jackie. "Are you . . . is your name Jackie?"

"Yes." Jackie turned to McGowan, who had re-entered the room zipping up a heavy blue windbreaker. Visible beneath the jacket was the outline of McGowan's shoulder holster. "Did she say anything about me?"

Bendix took the question. "She keeps saying, 'Tell Jackie!' Tell Jackie something.' "

"You know what that something would be, Ms. Walsh?" Mason asked sharply.

"No!" Jackie responded in kind.

"You a friend of hers?" Bendix asked, his question following just seconds after the last question of his partner.

"No," Jackie responded, her hands on her hips. "We have been associated in several ways, but we are definitely not friends."

"Well," Mason looked at his watch. "You got transportation, here?"

Jackie nodded.

"Why don't you get over to the hospital?" The policeman's suggestion was clearly meant to be an order. "You'd better hurry. The prognosis isn't good."

"Why would I do that?" Jackie asked at once.

Mason gave her a look. "Don't you think it's in your best interest, ma'am, to hear what your friend might say to you—or about you?"

"No," Jackie replied immediately. "And I've already told you she's not my friend." By this point Jackie was starting to get a little hot under the collar. "You know, Detective, it may be your job or your sworn duty to run around solving crimes. But it's not mine. I'm as anxious as anyone to be a good citizen in this town—but *I* will be the one to decide where my obligations begin and end."

McGowan put himself between the angry detective and the irate film professor. "Jackie, please. What Detective Mason is trying to ask you in his own clumsy way is, will you please help us out as a very valuable favor to your community by going down and listening to what Merida Green has to say?"

"Well . . ."

"You may be the only person she's willing to talk to," McGowan added softly.

Jackie was reluctant, but she was also curious. While she tried to make up her mind, McGowan turned to Detective Bendix. "I take it she hasn't said anything to us about what happened?"

Bendix shook his head.

McGowan looked at Jackie, saw that she would probably need some more convincing, then turned back to the stolid homicide detectives. "Mason, Bendix, go down to your car. I'll join you in a minute."

As soon as their footfalls faded to silence, McGowan turned back to Jackie. "Listen, I don't want to seem melo-dramatic about this, but if Con Mitchell was killed for the same reasons the others were killed, to shut them up, I may be the next one on their list."

"Why, Michael?" Jackie asked, alarm in her voice. "What do you know?"

"Nothing," McGowan quickly replied. "I swear it. But look at the chain. Dugan was Hopfelt's partner. When Hopfelt left to take the security job at the university, Dugan was partnered with Mitchell."

"So that's why Matt Dugan ended up with Jake," Jackie interrupted.

"Oh, sure," McGowan responded off-handedly. "I thought that was obvious. The only way a cop could get a section one discharge and end up with an A-1 canine to protect him was if he had friends in the right places."

Finally, something that had long bothered Jackie began to make sense. "That explains why Mitchell was always so irritable about us having Jake," Jackie realized. "He had to keep pretending that it wasn't his idea to give a valuable police dog to a drunk."

McGowan nodded, then added, "The thing is, Matt Dugan, drunk or sober, was a man whose life was in danger. I think Con was told whatever Matt knew. That's why he sacrificed his prize K-9. He had to."

"And how are you and Mitchell connected?" Jackie asked.

"When Dugan was discharged," McGowan replied, "I became his partner. Mitchell got more and more involved with the dogs—which I didn't find as interesting, frankly. So when I heard that there was a lieutenant's post open in the university precinct, I transferred over there so I could take the test. Mitchell and I were never that close and he never told me anything."

"Are you sure?"

"Pretty sure. And I don't think anyone, including me, ever made a connection between Matt Dugan and Danielle Sherman. But . . ."

"They might have thought you suspected something," Jackie supplied. "And, since generally you are considered an honest cop . . ."

"I certainly hope I'm considered an honest cop," McGowan answered. "I know I am one."

Jackie nodded. "Then why would you sit on what you knew all this time? According to their thinking."

McGowan shrugged. "We're speculating now. All right. Why? Maybe because I was biding my time. I've been making my way up the promotional ladder pretty quickly, they've got to figure. Sergeant in four years. Detective in six. Detective sergeant in seven. Lieutenant in ten. Captain in twelve. They know I know that the current commissioner is a political hack and that the last commissioner, Max

Greenaway, was thick as thieves with the Curtis administration. So maybe they think that it wouldn't have helped me at all to be the one insisting they reopen the Danielle Sherman investigation. It wouldn't have made anyone happy to show that maybe Matt Dugan wasn't any great undercover hero, but just a cop who couldn't control his alcohol."

Jackie nodded. This went right along the lines she had been thinking.

"No one," McGowan continued, "wants to remember Matt Dugan as just a beat cop who thought he had the goods on somebody but couldn't mount any kind of effective investigation to get them. If we're right, that's why the last time I was up for the captaincy, Commissioner Stillman derailed my promotion."

"But now you are a captain," Jackie pointed out.

"And I could—if I wanted to—reopen the investigation."

"But you can't talk to Con Mitchell or Walter Hopfelt anymore."

McGowan nodded again. "They've got to be worried, Jackie—if there really is a *they*—that I may be fixing to blackmail the current administration with what I know."

Jackie shook her head and shivered. "When is this going to end, Michael? Everytime we seem to come to the end of this Matt Dugan investigation, another door opens and we find the corruption goes even further than we could ever guess."

McGowan put his arms out and Jackie permitted herself to be hugged for a moment. "Don't worry. Not about me, anyway."

"You just told me to worry."

"I know. The truth is, the person I'm worried about is you."

"Why?" Jackie moved back a few steps.

"If they're worried I know something," McGowan went on to explain, "they might be worried that you know it too. That I told you what I suspected somewhere along the line. Hell, if I really did know something, I would have told you. Probably."

Jackie nodded, understanding. "Palmer's greatest amateur sleuth."

"That's what they tell me." McGowan took Jackie's small hands in his own long-fingered, surgeon's hands. "So you have to be careful, Jackie. And . . . I'd like you to let me be responsible for your protection."

"No," Jackie responded, gently removing her hands from his. "I have Jake."

"He didn't keep you from being knocked on the head the last time they wanted you out of the way," McGowan pointed out.

Jackie recalled the incident in question only too well. During the course of one of her amateur murder investigations, a man with a knife had knocked Jackie aside, then cut her dog.

McGowan had happened along and had quickly taken Jake inside. Then, while McGowan and her good friend Marcella had tended to her dog—tenderly nursing Jake, making him a warm bed, and then swiftly calling the vet and offering him an enormous bribe to make a housecall—Jackie had staggered inside unaided, and had fallen unhelped to the carpet with a concussion.

"Okay," Jackie coolly conceded. "I'll ask Chief Healy for some protection, then."

"Jackie."

"Mike . . . we are no longer involved." Jackie's eyes blazed. "You had your chance and frankly—you blew it."

"Jackie!"

"Save it!" Jackie backed away a few feet. "You've got places to be and apparently so do I. All right. I'll go down to Marx-Wheeler, Michael. I'll talk to Merida, if she wants to talk to me, and relay to the police whatever it is she tells me. I'll talk to Chief Healy about that, about protection, and about whatever other police problems I have from now on. I was with you long enough to appreciate how much proper procedure counts in the police department. And I don't want to see anyone get into trouble. Not even you. But don't embarrass us both, Michael, by asking me for anything else." Jackie then gathered up her belongings and headed for the door.

"Okay, whatever you say. I'll see you around then, Jackie," McGowan bitterly called out after her.

Jackie turned in the doorway. "I appreciate you helping me tonight, Michael. I'm flattered that you still want to sleep with me, and that you're still protective of me." After a beat, Jackie resumed in a more neutral voice. "And I miss you too. Sometimes. Especially when I'm alone in my house like I will be tonight. But that's not enough." Jackie looked deep into McGowan's eyes. "I don't know why your marriage broke up, Michael. But mine ended because of infidelity. You and I didn't have to get involved the way we did. I didn't think that I was ready for it and apparently you didn't either. But it happened. You pushed for it to happen. And you gave me your key. And then you let me embarrass myself that way, in front of my friend, walking into this apartment and finding you in bed with a woman who I also thought was my friend."

McGowan started to defend himself, but Jackie held up her hand to stop him. "I don't want to hear it. Really. This is not the swinging sixties, Michael. I am not nineteen years old. I don't want to sleep around and I don't want to share a bed with someone who does."

This really stung McGowan. "Oh, really?"

"Yes, really. And before you say it, whatever reputation Ron Dunn had before he met me, he's been faithful. How do I know? I just do. I felt there was something wrong with us months before I caught you in the act. And whenever I think I still have feelings for you, those other feelings come back and overwhelm me." Jackie regained control of herself and slowed down to a normal rhythm. "It would be convenient to have a boyfriend who lived here in Palmer. A nice guy, good lover, nice job, respected position in the community. Someone who gets along with my son and my dog. Someone who I share many happy memories with. But having a convenient relationship isn't enough for me either. I want to love and be loved. I want to trust and be trusted, and damn it, I want some respect! As long as Ron gives me that, I'll be with Ron."

Jackie started to become breathless. She paused for a moment to regain her composure, then decided she had said all she had to say.

McGowan tried several times to say something that would change her mind, but in the end, said only, "Let's go down to the basement and get your dogs then."

Jackie nodded. And then a tear squeezed out. It lingered for only a moment before a blink squashed it. Jackie had made her decision—there would be no more tears for Michael McGowan.

CHAPTER 11

Jackie's next stop was the Marx-Wheeler Medical Center.

The hospital building itself was a hybrid structure, a typical case of grafting new hospital wings onto old so as to keep patients and medical personnel perpetually tripping over construction equipment.

The redbrick "T" that made up the center part of Marx-Wheeler was all that was left of the Wheeler Facility for the Aging, a hospital originally founded by Quakers in 1833.

In the late 1970s, Mendel Marx, a television evangelist, "donated" two wings to the hospital in exchange for free health care for life for himself and his extended family. As Marx had elderly parents (who first became ill, it was said, when their son converted), seven sons, nine daughters-in-law (two of the Marx sons settled in Utah), and thirty-seven grandchildren, his seven-million-dollar donation turned out to be quite a bargain.

Since that time, Dick Bellamy, with a powerfully connected wife behind him, had managed to convince most of the town's millionaires, including Max Greenaway, the former police commissioner and current chairman of McKean Beverages (a division of McKean Pharmaceutical Industries), to donate everything from magnetic reasonance machines to hospital wings entirely devoted to people who weren't actually very sick, but needed to get away from the family a while and have people in white uniforms wait on them.

All in all, Marx-Wheeler was an odd hospital, Jackie thought to herself as she walked through the stone arch entrance. It was one of the few institutions in the country where the patients preferred the old section of the hospital to the new.

Strolling through the main lobby, Jackie was surprised to see her mother a few yards away, and shouted to get her attention. Frances Costello, resplendent as always in a turquoise pants suit, grabbed her chest and Lamaze-breathed for a moment.

"There's no case for killing me, Jacqueline Shannon,"— Frances gasped—"you've precious little waiting for you as an inheritance. Besides, of course, Victor who's worth his weight in gold. To me, anyway."

"Mom . . ." Jackie kissed her mother briefly on the cheek. "What are you doing here?"

"I'm going to put a fresh spray of wisteria in Maggie's bedside vase," Frances replied with an air of surprise that anyone could even ask such a question. "Ach. Anything you can do, if you know what I mean. It's like a prison ward up there. And thank you for finally coming . . ." Frances then gave Jackie a bear hug which turned into a good shaking as her emotions swung in a heartbeat from warm affection to outraged indignation. " . . . though I'd like to pinch two more holes in your ears for taking this long to do it. Maggie asks for you every day. I made excuses for you as long as I could, then finally I had to lie for you. Tell her you'd been by several times to say hi, but she was still groggy from her medication."

"I'm sorry, Mother," Jackie replied, genuinely contrite.

"And so you should be," Frances remarked approvingly. "You didn't bring any flowers, did you?"

Jackie shook her head guiltily.

"Good!" Frances exclaimed with a passion that was nearly unseemly. "They won't let any flowers in the hospital unless they're bought at their own florist's shop here—very expensive, I might add. They'll give you a lot of doubletalk about germs if you ask them. But they aren't fooling a soul! They're nothing but a bunch of money-grubbing IRA gestapos, if you ask me!" Frances's penetrating voice carried throughout the lobby, momentarily drowning out the sound of an approaching ambulance siren.

The burly security guard Dan Ditko, a former policeman who was harrassed off the force for answering 911 calls so fast it embarrassed his fellow officers, was by this point in his career simply bored by people yelling dire imprecations against the hellhole in which he worked. His only response, therefore, was to yawn widely.

"Cover your mouth why don't you!" Frances yelled, when she saw him.

"All right, Mother," Jackie quickly interjected. "I'll buy the wisteria spray and meet you upstairs in a few moments."

Frances smiled, then grabbed Jackie's arm in a death grip. "I'll stand with you, dear. We can wait a minute. It's so damn depressing up there."

"All the more reason," Jackie replied, disengaging herself with some difficulty, "why you should go up there and keep her company until I get there. Maggie's the one that's dying, Mother. I'm sure she's a lot more depressed than you are."

"Well, there's some justice in that," Frances conceded. "I'll go up then. You come as fast as you can. Once they serve dinner, you can't hear yourself thinking, what with all the complaining and the nurses' aides standing around waiting to be tipped. Now you know where she is, don't you? Of course you don't. It's ward seven, fourth floor. Can you remember that?"

"Yes, Mother," Jackie responded, hugging Frances and giving her another quick kiss on the cheek.

"Well, say," Frances beamed, "you're affectionate today." Frances turned to the security guard. "Did you see how my daughter kissed me just now?"

Ditko gave her a flat-eyed look.

"Well, when was the last time you kissed your mother?"

"This morning," the guard snarled.

"Well, good," Frances replied. She turned back to Jackie. "I can't begin to tell you how nice these public displays of affection would be if only you didn't smell so thoroughly of dog. What, have you been taking cooking lessons from that Asian friend of yours from the poker game?"

"Mother!" Jackie exclaimed. It was a constant battle to keep her mother from airing her very 1940s beliefs and prejudices. "Suki does not cook dog and if you'll recall, I have two of my own."

"Ah, yes." Frances shrugged, not really very interested. "Whatever. I tend to forget that there are other pets in the world besides big beautiful odorless snakes." Frances was pleased to see that the mother-kissing security guard was now hanging on her every word. "Your father, you know, he was always trying to get me a dog, even though I kept telling him not to. So he buys me some ugly little South American dingus. Some sort of Chiwa-thing. Little legs. Smooth in the front, bushy in the back. I hate to tell you what that looked like."

Jackie and the security guard both blushed. Frances shook her head. "Awful lewd-looking thing."

"Mother!" Jackie protested weakly, knowing that everyone in the lobby was now eavesdropping on their conversation.

Frances groaned as if whacked with an oar and threw her hands in the air in supplication. "And now here it comes. Wait for it. She can't bear to talk a moment with her dear white-haired mother. For two years they live off you, listening to every word you say while they're suckling the milk from your breast, but then the moment they can handle a toddler bottle, it's the last you ever see of them."

Crimson with embarrassment, Jackie avoided the eyes of the snickering security guard and escaped into the florist shop, her mother calling after her, "Sure, run away. I'll be here soon enough as a customer. You won't hear a word from me then as they slowly tug the dingy white sheet over my head . . . !"

The hairnet-wearing florist shop worker gave Jackie a sympathetic look. "Did she send you in here to buy the wisteria spray for her friend?"

Jackie nodded weakly.

"I'll pick you a good one," the florist lady offered. "I know how critical she can be. *Believe me*, I know."

Jackie was reaching for her wallet when she suddenly saw Doctor Richard Bellamy passing. "Dick!" she cried loudly.

Bellamy blushed and looked around for his heckler.

Jackie threw some money down on the counter, picked up the wisteria spray, and rushed out into the corridor. "Dick, hi! Can I have a word with you?"

"I suppose so," Bellamy replied nervously. "Could we chat as we walk to my office?"

"Sure," Jackie responded, falling into step with him. "How's Jane?"

"My wife the mayor grows stronger every day," Bellamy answered hollowly. "It'll take a drug stronger than interferon to stop her."

"That's great," Jackie replied, somewhat at a loss for the right words to respond to that one.

"Here visiting relatives, I don't hope?" Bellamy inquired,

nodding his head toward the wisteria spray.

"No," Jackie responded, stepping aside to avoid two orderlies playing hockey in the hallway with a couple of crutches and a balled up piece of surgical adhesive tape. "Actually I'm here to see two people."

"Not a suicide love pact, I hope." Bellamy commented, sliding his access card through the slot reader of the VIP elevator. "We see a lot of that here and it's always so sad. A team is definitely no asset when it comes to a well-planned suicide."

"Actually, no, Dr. Bellamy," Jackie shouted over a P.A. announcement asking a Doctor Michalowski to move his double-parked Maserati so a disaster van could pull up to the emergency room doors. "I'm hoping to talk to Merida Green!"

"Oh." Bellamy shuddered—never a good sign. "I hear she's badly burned, you know. Charred, practically. We're doing the best we can for her, of course, but . . ." Bellamy made a deprecating hand gesture, showing just how little that was worth.

"Apparently she wants to talk to me personally," Jackie answered, as they got on the elevator.

"Well, then"—Bellamy reached absently through the pockets of his white smock, coming up only with a silver flask and the receipt from his forty-dollar luncheon—"I'd better write you a pass to get by the security guard. Some of those young minimum-wage fellows we hire are just plain crazy. Wyatt Earps, the lot of them." Bellamy then dropped his voice and went on to confide, "Just as soon put a bullet in your back as look at you."

As they got on the elevator, Jackie couldn't help but notice the strong odor of blackberry brandy on the veteran physician's breath.

"Seat?" he offered.

Jackie noticed for the first time that the elevator was equipped with a small love-seat bench. In answer to Jackie's look, Bellamy responded, "One thing you learn on this job is to sit down whenever they'll let you. I'd hate to show you my varicose veins. Like the paneling?"

Jackie tapped the elevator's right wall with her nails. "Real wood."

"Absorbs sound!" Bellamy exclaimed. "Notice how quietly we're moving? Don't hear a whisper from the works."

Jackie gave the doctor a look, then pointed out mildly, "Actually, Dick, I think you still have to push your floor number."

"Right you are," Bellamy responded with perfect aplomb. The good doctor had made far too many errors in his career to be flustered by such a harmless mistake. "Anyway, we're trying to enjoy what few luxuries the state regulatory agencies reluctantly leave us." As Bellamy talked, he adjusted his tie in the elevator's platinum-framed mirror. "Mark my words, if Congress forces a national health insurance plan on us, we'll be lucky to afford a rusty pocketknife for surgery and a bottle of cheap gin for an anesthetic."

"Food for thought," Jackie said, using her favorite noncommittal answer. She then followed Bellamy into his gala suite of offices.

As they passed a surprisingly competent-looking security guard, Jackie asked, "Have you hired a personal bodyguard?"

"No, no." Bellamy pooh-poohed. "I get a few death threats when patients find out how much they've been charged for aspirin, but by the time we're through with them, they're not in any condition to mount much of an attack. Frankly, let's face it, er . . ."

"Jackie."

"Jackie, right. Like the former first lady." Bellamy started to laugh at his own joke, but then forgot what it was. "Er, what was I saying?"

"You were saying something about . . ."

"Oh, yes. What's her name. Treated her second husband, you know. Thought we had his illness well under control, then poof. Ah well, you've got to take the bad with the good on this job."

Jackie nodded, wondering what the good part was.

"Jeffries out there," Bellamy continued, "is from the city's security staff. Keeps an eye on me, because I am, after all, married to the mayor. Sort of a special secret service spousal protection deal. You know, like Bess Truman used to get."

Bellamy opened the door to his office and Jackie stepped in, feeling herself sink into the extremely rare double-deep Persian rug. "Wow!"

"Careful you don't turn an ankle," Bellamy warned. "Our fracture ward's a veritable charnel house these days."

Jackie shielded her eyes as she contemplated the physician's bulging display cases. "My goodness. This is like a museum."

Bellamy nodded, and then wiped his large red nose with a silk handkerchief. "Actually, much of this junk came from the Palmer Gallery. The curator, nice fellow, had to have a gallbladder out last year. And you know the complications that come after a gallbladder."

"Isn't that beautiful," Jackie remarked, pointing to a small, beautifully executed Braque hanging next to Bellamy's framed diploma from the North Dakota School of Medicine.

"Yes. But don't whisper a word about that to the French government. They don't know I have it, you see," Bellamy instructed. "One hates to deal with black-market criminals, of course, but you just know that if you don't buy it, it'll fall into the hands of some Greek shipping tycoon who'll just put it out on his yacht. Terrible thing. Do you have any idea what salt water spray does to an oil painting?"

"No, but it's food for thought, I guess," Jackie declared uncomfortably.

"I know. You're anxious to talk with Ms. Green." Bellamy stepped over to the intercom. "Carruthers, this is Dr. Bellamy. Alert the staff in the burn center that Ms. Green is about to receive a visitor. Give her a slug of epinephrine, dexadrine, whatever you think appropriate."

Bellamy clicked off the intercom. "Bronwyn Carruthers, my assistant. Isn't an M.D., but I trust his judgment on most medical matters far more than I trust my staff. Brandy?"

"No, thank you," Jackie responded, noticing how badly Bellamy's hands shook as he clutched the bottle.

"Sure? This cask was laid down the year this town was founded, in 1807." Bellamy saw Jackie shake her head in polite refusal once again. "Suit yourself. To history! And we all know what history is. Bunk!" Bellamy then knocked back a snort and a half. He continued babbling in order to cover the fact that he was pouring a second drink, bigger than the first. "Have you seen the portraits in City Hall of old Pirate Palmer? What a sense of humor, eh? Having himself painted as if he were some Revolutionary War hero receiving a land grant from the British. Rather an impossibility, wouldn't you say? Especially when you remember that there were only thirteen colonies altogether by the time the British left our scabrous shores for good. I suppose City Hall doesn't like to remind the citizenry that this town was named after a man who gained possession of the downtown area by backshooting some poor son-of-a-bitch in an ambush."

Jackie fell back on a response which had been a favorite of H. L. Mencken. "You may be right."

Bellamy poured himself two more fingers of brandy and then sat down heavily in his desk chair. "Would you like to sit for a moment?" Bellamy offered, pointing to a red velour-covered armchair.

"No, thank you," Jackie refused politely. "I really should be going."

"Really?" Bellamy seemed disappointed. "You don't want to ask me if Ms. Green set the blast that killed her paramour herself?"

Jackie's mouth opened in surprise. "Do you mean you can actually determine that?"

"Well, no. I don't think we can. But that seemed like the sort of question you might ask." Bellamy ran his hand through his spiky white peroxided hair. "You always ask such good questions. Or so I thought. I was sitting here preparing to be grilled for hours."

At that moment the City Hall secret-service man, Dannen Jeffries, stuck his head in the door. "Doctor Bellamy, there's a scrub nurse here to see you, sir."

Bellamy quickly reached for a pad and scribbled a pass for Jackie. "Well, Ms. Walsh. Thanks for stopping by."

"Thank you," Jackie replied, taking the slip of paper.

"That's what we're here for." Bellamy smiled toothily. "If I could just impose on you to go out *that* door."

Jackie exited through the side door and wondered as she descended in the special elevator just how much the mayor knew of her husband's nefarious doings. One of the things that had led to the downfall of the previous mayor— Danielle's father Big Bill Curtis—was his very publicly disintegrating marriage which came apart just before Mickey Farrow testified before the grand jury and the federal indictments were handed down.

It was no wonder, Jackie decided, that the mayor had decided to overcome some of the very negative publicity associated with her husband by coming out in favor of a relatively popular cause, the early pardoning of Merida Green.

Passing through one group of bereaved visitors after another, Jackie eventually found her way to the burn ward where Merida Green was resting. When she walked into the room Jackie saw a familiar person standing near the bed.

"Nancy!"

"Jackie!" Nancy Gordon, estranged wife of the city's medical examiner, turned toward her friend with a big smile. "How are you?"

"I'm fine," Jackie smiled, rubbing her hand across her brow. "I'm dead tired, actually. And it's hot in here, isn't it?"

"Yes," the lovely Hispanic pianist replied. "She's burning up."

Jackie followed Nancy's eyes toward the heavily gauze-wrapped patient in the single bed.

"Merida, are you awake?" Nancy said in rapid Spanish.

Jackie was amazed. "I didn't know Merida was . . ."

"She was born Merida Verde," Nancy explained. "What, you thought maybe she was Jewish with a nice tan?"

"Something like that." Jackie smiled. "How did you get involved with this?"

"I volunteer here two afternoons a week," Nancy replied.

Jackie wondered, but did not ask if that was a new development which had occurred since the trial separation from her husband had begun.

"You see," Nancy continued, "how my afternoon's turned out to be."

"How is she?" Jackie asked softly.

"I don't know," Nancy confessed. "The nurse went to lie down a couple of hours ago and I've been here ever since. No one has really told me anything, except that I should keep my ears open in case she makes any statements."

"Has she?"

"She occasionally sings in her sleep," Nancy said softly. "Spanish nursery songs. Choked me up, Jackie. Tell you the truth, I haven't heard those songs since I was a little girl."

Jackie saw the fatigue in Nancy's eyes and urged her, "Why don't you go home? If you see a nurse, send her in. I can hang out for an hour or so."

"Okay. Do you know any Spanish?"

"I have that Linda Ronstadt album," Jackie replied.

"Well, we'll hope she talks in English then. Goodbye." Nancy put on her sweater and was about to leave when she decided to ask one more thing. "Jackie?"

Jackie, who had been looking through her shoulder bag for a notebook, looked up. "Yes?"

"Would you like to come over for dinner some time?" Nancy smiled sadly, then added, "It's rather lonely with Cosmo gone and Katharina-Elena away at school. I love to cook, but I feel kind of silly just doing it for myself."

"I'd love to." Jackie smiled. "Sometime next week, maybe?"

Nancy smiled happily. "I'll give you a call." The two women exchanged brief hugs and then, as Nancy departed, Jackie walked over to the visitor's chair and prepared to sit down.

A voice immediately came from the bed. "Is she gone?"

Startled, Jackie answered slowly, "Yes."

Merida Green's eyes snapped open. "I thought she'd never leave. What kept you?"

Jackie bristled. "Maybe I haven't made this plain enough, Merida. I am not a policewoman. I am not at anyone's beck and call, except for maybe my family who see less of me than anyone."

"Oh, please, please excuse me, Jackie," Merida replied

sarcastically. "I guess being blown up in a building made me a little testy. I don't expect you to understand."

Jackie, despite herself, apologetically asked, "How are you, Merida?"

As if by way of answer, Merida started pulling off her gauze bandages.

Jackie was shocked. "What are you doing?"

Merida waved away Jackie's query. "I'm fine. They found me covered with soot, and the herbal compress I always wear to bed, and thought I had third-degree burns. Idiots. *I* added the bandages once I got here so I didn't have to talk to the police. I wanted to talk to you."

"Why?" Jackie asked quickly.

"I want to tell you something."

"Yes?"

"I didn't kill Con Mitchell," Merida stated firmly. "Look at my eyes, Jackie. I loved that man, warts and all. I might have knifed him in an argument, but a bomb in his police radio is definitely not my style."

Jackie sat down heavily in the only visitor's chair. A bomb! This case grew more and more complicated by the moment and she hadn't even begun to write the introductory remarks about *Invasion of the Body Snatchers* she had planned to deliver to her film lab!

"Jackie . . . Still with me?"

Jackie nodded. "I'm just surprised, that's all. Are you sure that's what happened?"

"It must be," Merida replied. "We were in the bedroom. Con couldn't sleep." Merida threw back the sheets on her bed. "He said he was going into the living room to do some paperwork. I knew what that meant."

Jackie watched fascinated as Merida pulled out her intravenous line, placed an alcohol swab in the crook of her arm, then pressed her forearm tightly to her bicep, waiting for the wound to close. "What did it mean?"

"Con had gotten into the habit of having a couple of cans of beer before going to sleep," Merida explained, her voice calm and measured. "He knew I didn't approve, so I heard him go into the kitchen, then come out and turn on the radio."

"To drown out the sound of him opening the can?" Jackie asked.

"Probably." Merida shrugged. "Or he may have just wanted to hear a few minutes of police calls. They find it soothing. What about your lieutenant? Did he listen to the police band before he fell asleep?"

"No," Jackie answered absently. "Actually Michael has one of those wave machines. You know, with the water."

Merida smiled widely.

Jackie blushed, first because she had admitted that she had spent the night with McGowan in his apartment, and second, to be speaking so familiarly to a woman she barely knew. Not to mention a murderer.

Merida got up and started for the door.

"Where do you think you're going?" Jackie asked.

"To find the she-cat who killed my fiancé." Merida's eyes blazed with what seemed to be righteous indignation. "I've got to know, Jackie, whether she was trying to kill him or me."

Jackie followed Merida out the door. "She?" she asked. "How do you know it's a she?"

"I'll tell you when I get dressed. Do you have your Jeep here?"

"What about the nurse?" Jackie asked.

"Do you have your Jeep here?" Merida demanded. "Yes or no?"

"Yes!"

"Good!" Merida clapped her hands together with satisfaction. "The nurse has been drugged. Follow me."

CHAPTER 12

Merida led Jackie to a little room just off the nursing station which said, "Chart Room." Inside, a nurse in a white uniform sat in an upright wooden chair, sound asleep and snoring heavily.

"Goodness," Merida complained, making a beeline for the cubicle on the south wall which held her clothing. "What a racket."

Jackie felt bad for the woman. Perhaps it was the drug that was making her snore so raucously. "How did you dope her?"

"Sleeping pills," Merida answered with a negligent shrug. "Pain pills. I begged for all I could get, then slipped them into her McKean Carrot Soda."

"You're lucky she didn't pass out somewhere the security cameras could see her," Jackie commented.

"Luck had nothing to do with it," Merida snarled. "I noticed when they brought me in that Nurse Thunder over there was taking a break in this room. So I dosed her light enough so it wouldn't take effect for a few minutes. That way I knew she'd come back here and pass out."

Jackie was impressed despite herself. She considered herself to be a fairly intelligent person who met challenges head on, but she did tend to procrastinate on things at times, and when it came to doling out precise measures of Mickey Finns or poisons, forget it.

"Worked like a charm, and the best part is, because she was complaining about having to work a double shift to that quack Bellamy, they'll think her being out like a light is natural. I'll tell you one thing, though. It's a good thing I'm not really sick. Between the snoozing nurses and the doctors who sneak by when they know you're asleep or in the bathroom and then bill you later for a consultation, and the bedbugs and the dripping ceilings and the drugs bought at surplus sales that have turned yellow from age, you'd get better care if you passed out in a barbershop."

Jackie watched as the paroled murderess tied the wide cloth belt of a shapeless blue dress. All that kept going through Jackie's mind was, *I bought a dress just like that recently. Does it make me look hippy too?*

"Jackie."

"What?"

"Are you ready to go?"

"Just a minute. A question or two first, if you don't mind."

"Shoot."

"Why is the head of the hospital keeping up on your case?" Jackie asked. "That doesn't sound routine."

"I wouldn't be surprised if he came by to press a pillow over my face," Merida responded. "The Bellamys aren't any better than the Curtises, Jackie. Believe me."

"I think I'm beginning to find that out," Jackie responded. "Did you know that the police sent me here to find out what your statement was? What do you think is going to happen when they find you've gone?"

"I couldn't care less. I haven't done anything wrong. They want to arrest me, they'll have to find me first."

"If they do suspect you of setting the bomb yourself, this running out is going to look suspicious as hell."

"You overestimate the local constabulary, Jackie," Merida scoffed. "Maybe you or I would be capable of that kind of linear thinking, but the people the Palmer police get these days can barely fill out their applications. If they don't find me here, they'll just figure the hospital knocked off another patient."

"Really, Merida . . ."

"Enough already." Merida Green slipped on her second brown low-heeled shoe (which really didn't go with the dress). "Look, we don't have time to argue. If whoever's killing ex-Palmer policemen isn't afraid of them, why should we be? We'll get out of here, you'll tell me what you know. I'll tell you what I know. If I decide I can really trust you."

"What's that supposed to mean?" Jackie asked, folding her arms.

"It means you don't like me," Merida answered matter-of-factly. "That's obvious. Before I got out of prison I didn't like you. Now I'm trying real hard."

Despite herself, Jackie smiled.

Merida marched toward the door, clearly expecting Jackie to follow her. "Come, come. The sooner we solve this case, the sooner we can go back to our boring cerebral lives."

Seeing Merida's point, Jackie followed her out into the hall. They passed the framed pastel drawings of Doctor Bellamy's yacht (which he thought might add a cheery nautical flavor to the burn ward) and got as far as the elevator. Jackie, like Merida, wearing a long, floor-length white cotton scrub gown that they had taken from a supply closet, saw her reflection in the mirror and ran her fingers through her hair, trying to fluff up the top.

"What are you doing?" Merida asked incredulously. "You're not supposed to look beautiful, Jackie."

"It's not that," Jackie replied, still fussing. "It's just that it gets flat on top."

"Good. Cover it with this." Merida pulled a paper bonnet that looked like a shower cap out of her pocket.

"Before I do," Jackie replied, taking the cap, "Why is it I have to dress up like a nurse? It's okay if *I* walk out of the hospital, remember?"

"Not if you're exiting with someone who isn't supposed to leave," Merida reminded her. "You're a familiar face, Jackie. You've been seen on TV. Everyone knows you're here to see me, the terrible killer. So if you go out with a nurse in scrub clothes, averting her face, who is that going to fool? Do you want to get in trouble?"

"No," Jackie responded, tucking her hair up under the hat. "I just wish we could do this without looking like Laverne and Shirley."

"Now, see. I would have said Lucy and Ethel," responded Merida. "Shows you how quickly generation gaps form these days."

The two uneasy allies traveled to the first floor in the elevator, got off, and were walking to the parking lot when all of a sudden they were spotted.

Charles "Bingo" Allen, a dour beat reporter for the *Chronicle*, was hanging out by the emergency room door with his television contemporary Drew Feigl, when they saw Jackie and Merida. With just a glimpse at their faces, Feigl couldn't be sure who they were. But Bingo Allen could spot them a mile away. Thumbing his Stetson fedora up on his head, Allen exclaimed loudly, "*Say!* Isn't that Merida Green?"

"It sure is," Feigl said quickly. "And who's that with her?"

"What, are you blind?" Bingo exclaimed. "That's Marcella's friend Jackie Walsh, Palmer's ace amateur sleuth."

"You mean the one with the dog? Hey, you!" Feigl yelled, startling a nearby stabbing victim whose life force was slowly ebbing away as the charge nurse waited for the patient's credit card to be verified. "Stop!"

Jackie and Merida were out through the dangerous revolving doors in an instant and burst out into the parking lot.

"Jake!" Jackie yelled. "Maury! Where are you?"

Maury responded first, galloping out to meet his mistress, holding in his mouth a big strip of a tire he had ripped off someone's parked bicycle.

Jake appeared a few moments later from a different direction, as if wanting to disassociate himself from the bumptious one-year-old.

"Where to?" Jackie asked Merida, tearing off her "Protect-a-Cap" and giving it to Maury to tear to pieces.

"How about," Merida proposed, "the scene of the crime?"

"*Locus en quo*," Jackie translated knowledgeably.

"Very good. You've been talking to Dean Westfall," Merida cracked, referring to Rodgers University's dean of faculty, a thin man with leathery skin, a tight-lipped smile, and a habit of making jokes nobody understood.

"No, I got that from a bartender," Jackie replied, giving Maury a little kick to help him squeeze into the back seat. "Back to the Circus Maximus again, huh, fellows?"

"No, Jackie," Merida corrected her. "I don't know anything about that case. I'm talking about where Walter Hopfelt died . . ."

"The Sabin Hughes wing of Armstong Hall," Jackie responded.

Merida nodded and familiarly reached out to scratch Maury behind his ears. "Let's boogie."

CHAPTER 13

B. Crowder Westfall held his wrist and counted his pulse as he waited for someone to pick up. The dean's veins and arteries were cracking like high-tension wires and the fact that he had been on hold with the police department for five minutes did nothing to bring it under control. "This is really absurd," Westfall said to himself. "The Greeks built Persepolis in the time it takes these fools to pick up their phone." The elderly dean had been trying to get through to Chief Healy for several days now to report a very important thing he had seen from his office window while working late a few nights before.

"Damn, you idiots!" Dean Westfall mumbled, loosening his collar so the veins in his neck would have more room to throb. Where were they all? Out filling their balloon bellies with chocolate-dipped donuts, most likely. Was it really a coincidence the Muzak on the hold line sounded just like a *101 Strings* orchestration of the *Double Donuts* theme?

Finally, a heavily accented voice came back on the line. "University Police Precinct, Sergeant Vasayanvidnivich speaking."

A little startled, Dean Westfall sputtered, "I want to speak to Healy. That is to say, Chief Lorne Healy. He's in homicide."

"You wish to report a homicide?" the recent hiree, fresh off the jet from Vladivostok, asked.

Westfall sighed. He knew it was important to be patient with these well-meaning immigrants of what had once been Communist East Europe. And he was thrilled that the sergeant, one of the same people he had been taught since a small boy to hate, fear, and despise, had beaten out an American job applicant, fair and square (or perhaps as a result of a marvelously legislated quota bill), and was now working in the police department, handing out judgment to arch-conservative, American Legion–run Palmer. But why on God's green earth did they have to hire one with such rudimentary language skills—that is to say, an English-challenged individual—as a dispatcher?

"Hello. Is it still there?" the voice asked.

"Yes." Westfall sighed. "I'm still here, Sergeant. Listen to me, please. I have some information that I think is related to a homicide. Are you with me, so far? And you—not you personally, but you the police—have a department in your building called homicide. Now I want to be connected with the homicide department or whatever other department you have which handles violent crimes. I can't for the life of me understand why you don't just have a violent crimes division, but I'm sure there are all sorts of official police union foot-dragging regulations against it. I don't know and frankly, at this point in my life, I am too old to waste any more time in fanciful speculations. I do know that if you still have a policeman or two hanging around who could actually beat up a small child without some sort of automatic weapon, I would have that sort of uniformed officer out on the street. Walking a beat, instead of stapling paperwork in triplicate. If I were in charge, I would put only the cream of the cream in the violent crimes division, since that after all is why we should have police in the first

place. To protect the helpless from violent crimes! The rest
of the force, the deadbeats, donut-dunkers, alcoholics, and
timeservers could go over to the automobile and home bur-
glaries investigation department, where people only pretend
to do police work."

"Yes, sir," Vasayanvidnivich replied, writing furiously in
Russian.

"After all," Dean Westfall continued, by now so deep
in his fantasy of reforming the police department that he
had almost forgotten the original purpose of his phone call,
"sometimes the evil inflicted upon the living is far worse
than the quick, painless death visited on the uncaring dead.
I'm not speaking of the obvious, brutal rapes, mutilations,
and muggings that leave once-intelligent humans dithering
hulks. Mind you, I'm talking about those who watch a man
murdered before their eyes . . ."

Hopelessly confused with what the dean was saying to
him, the Russian sergeant gave up and connected Westfall
to homicide.

"Hello, Chief Healy."

"Finally!"

"What can I do for you, Mr. Finally?"

"No, you idiot. I'm calling from Rodgers University and
I have some information on a homicide you're working
on. It's something I saw a few days ago . . . wait." Dean
Westfall suddenly saw something outside the window. Peer-
ing through the blinds, the elderly Greek classicist saw a
sight just too frightening for his poor heart to bear.

At the same time, at the University precinct house, hearing only the clatter of a cheap plastic phone receiver hitting
the floor, Chief Healy charged out of his narrow office
into the harshly lit halls, and demanded of those lining
the corridor, "What the hell was that?"

Officer Sanji guiltily put down the powdered-sugar shaker and asked, "What's the matter, Chief?"

Healy shouted up to the dispatcher's station, which was on a raised platform above the din of the other phones. "Vasily, what did the caller want?"

"Couldn't get a word out of him. He didn't seem to want to talk to anyone but you, Chief," the dispatcher lied.

"Damn. Our one good lead in two weeks and it slips through our fingers."

If the other policemen in the room shared Healy's chagrin that a dangerous murderer still walked the streets, they concealed it perfectly.

"Okay. Listen," Healy instructed. "The line's still open. Put a trace on it."

As the dispatcher reached for his manual to figure out how such a thing could be done, the homicide chief turned to Officer Sanji. "Muhammed, you and Watson get over to the university ASAP. He mentioned the university, right, Sergeant?"

The dispatcher smiled and nodded, without really understanding the question.

"That's what I thought." Healy then turned back to Officer Sanji, still slowly putting the lid on an over-lightened coffee. "What the hell are you still doing here, Mo?"

Officer Sanji saluted. "Me and Watson to Asap Street. Yes, sir. Right away. I didn't know it was important, sir."

Healy threw his hat to the floor in frustration. "Asap isn't a street, you idiot! It's police talk. It means 'As soon as possible.' Are you with me now, Corporal? It means 'Go.' It means 'Move it!' It means 'Pronto!' "

"Ah, yes sir," Sanji nodded, at last understanding. "You mean, sir, 'Quick as the Ganges River flows.' I leave at once."

CHAPTER 14

Far from all the noise and confusion that passed for police work, Jackie and Merida, still in their ghostly white surgical scrub gowns, picked the lock of the Sabin Hughes Annex and quickly vanished inside.

Led by the two big dogs, the amateur sleuth and paroled murderess proceeded to the storage area behind the main stairs where Hopfelt had met the floor with disastrous results to both.

By now all the police paraphernalia had been removed and the only traces of what had happened was the new, dark brown uncured cement substitute replacing the section of floor that had been damaged.

Leaving Merida to hold onto the frisky Maury's harness, Jackie and Jake sniffed around. Jackie watched tensely as Jake investigated every corner and then turned back, shaking his aquiline head.

"Anything?" Merida asked.

"No. Of course the place has probably been scrubbed clean," Jackie explained.

Merida nodded. "It's like I told you before, Jackie. There's no guarantee the murderess came down here to gloat over the body. What's the point? I wouldn't do it."

"You wouldn't?" Jackie asked.

The two women locked eyes for a moment and then

Merida chuckled. "Oh, so I'm still a suspect, am I?"

"No," Jackie admitted. "Not really. I admit it, there doesn't seem to be any way you could have killed Hopfelt."

"Well, thank goodness for small favors." Suddenly Merida, her hand still on the leash, was jerked off balance. "I am going to kill this dog, however."

Jackie motioned her quiet. "Wait a minute, I think Maury smells something."

"Oh. Is that what it is?" Merida looked down at the dog with something resembling helplessness. "What should I do?"

"Let him have his head a moment," Jackie instructed.

Merida let the lead slip loosely through her hand but did not release it completely. The elephant mastiff mongrel immediately went over to the corner and gobbled up a bit of cruller, obviously left there by a policeman.

"That reminds me," Merida cracked. "We should stop soon for dinner. I didn't have any of the hospital food, knowing that would finish me for sure."

Jackie ignored Merida's joke as she cocked her ear toward a sound in the distance. "Do you hear sirens?" she asked.

"After a year and a half in prison, I hear them in my sleep," Merida snapped. Then seeing Jackie's serious expression, she responded, "Sorry. No, I don't hear anything. But that's not to say there isn't something to hear. Rice Hill Penitentiary was a noisy place. My hearing still hasn't returned to normal."

"All right. Never mind," Jackie decided. "Maury!" The big puppy returned to Jackie's side and gave her hand a sloppy lick, both to be friendly and also to see if she was holding any treats. "Let's go upstairs."

At the same time, leaving Officer Sanji downstairs to make sure no one stole the police car, Officer Patrice

Watson, a solid, no-nonsense uniformed police officer, made her way to the dean of faculty's office in the Armstrong Building. There Watson found Dean Westfall sprawled on his carpet.

She immediately pulled the rug from the other end to flatten out the sharp folds. Patrice Watson could still hear the echo of her mother's long-ago words of wisdom: "Sharp folds are disastrous for those expensive Iranese rugs."

After making certain the carpet was all right, Watson then leaned down and put her ear to the dean of faculty's chest. "Can you hear me?" she yelled.

Westfall cringed and choked out a few words.

"Say again," Watson ordered, sliding her way up the dean's chest until her ear was very near his lips.

The dean groaned in pain and Officer Watson realized what was happening and removed her earring. "What is it, Dean? Talk to me. You seem to have had a heart attack."

The dean nodded.

"Good. We're on the same page, then." Watson had been an honors student in Community Communications at the Academy.

The dean repeated his previous mumbles.

"What's that? Ampersand? No, amber sand. A special kind of sand. No ambulate . . . Ambulance! You want an ambulance? Right! Good thinking," Watson tapped Westfall's thrombotic chest in approval and then stood up. She took a minute to put her earring back on and then opened the window. "Mo! Where are you?"

Watson saw the empty police car below, parked beneath one of Rodgers University's mighty oaks. She did not, however, see any signs of Officer Sanji.

"Damn," Watson exclaimed, stepping over the wheezing dean (who was desperately trying to elevate himself in case someone eventually came along who knew CPR) and strolled over to the telephone. "Now what's the emergency ambulance number?"

Watson struggled to remember. It had been months since she called it last. "Well, just have to call information, I guess," Officer Watson decided. She put the receiver to her ear, grimaced, and then once again removed her earring.

Meanwhile, in the Sabin Hughes Annex, Jackie and her party were making their way up the wide central stairway to the second floor. Jackie had brought her flashlight in from the Jeep, and there was some light coming in from the single-bulb ceiling fixture, but the group had to move slowly and carefully. Jackie would have liked to have Jake leading the way, but the intelligent Alsatian was still investigating a post of the wide handrail below her.

Jackie climbed to the top step and then—all of a sudden— saw a wild-eyed woman rush toward her, arm upraised. Jackie screamed. The woman's arm came down and Jackie could see she was pointing past her to Merida Green.

"You!" the woman shouted accusatively.

Merida saw, as Jackie played her flashlight on the accusing woman's face, a familiar countenance. "Hello, Alice," she said.

It was indeed Alice Blue, the wild-eyed housewife who had adopted Merida Green's freedom as her personal *raison d'être*, and who had by now become a publicity junkie. Ever since Merida had been freed, depriving Alice of a media pack hanging on her every word, the determined activist without a cause had decided to emulate Jackie and become an amateur sleuth, solving crimes throughout Palmer.

"Why haven't you called me, Merida?" the creepy, wild-haired housewife demanded. "I had a victory barbecue scheduled. Vegetarian, of course. To celebrate your return. You didn't even show up for your own 'Welcome Home' party. You humiliated everybody."

"I'm sorry, Alice . . ." Merida began.

But Alice cut her off ruthlessly. "Sorry doesn't cut it, Merida. Everyone just sort of trickled away and I haven't seen them since. We had an organization that could have done any amount of good and it all slipped through our fingers like ten dollars' worth of potter's sand."

Alice's husband Ford owned a hardware store, so her accusations tended to be product-specific.

"Come, come, Alice," Merida protested reasonably. "What good could the group have done, really?"

"Well, we could have gotten some of our other sisters out of prison, for one thing," Alice responded.

"Well, I don't mind helping out sisters, Alice," Merida replied. "But I'm not sure if I want to help out killers."

"So? Isn't that what you are, Merida?"

Merida was stunned into silence. Jackie felt her own ears burning with anger and resentment. "Do you mean to tell me, Alice Blue, that you started this whole publicity campaign to free Merida Green even though you knew she really had killed Philip Barger?"

"Oh, did I surprise Palmer's premier sleuth?" Alice sneered. "How wonderful for me. Yes, Jackie. That's exactly what I did. Times have changed, dear. If everyone else is going to go on one of those cheap, syndicated docudrama programs, tell some outrageous lie, and then reap the benefits, why shouldn't I?" Alice, of course, referred to programs like Jerry Waring's popular *Cry For the Victims* show.

"Ever since our bank went out of business," Alice continued, "we've been paying double the old interest to the new Golden Triangle Mortgage holders. Ford's store needed the boost and my little campaign helped, I'm happy to say."

Now it was Jackie's turn to be appalled into silence and for Merida to take a higher moral tone. "How could you possibly stoop to something so odious?"

Alice responded derisively, her hands on her hips. "Yes, right, Merida. And Alma Hitchcock really directed all of Alfred's films."

This stung the entirely academic authoress. "If you would read the book carefully, you would see how I constructed my hypothesis brick by brick until—"

"—you had an outhouse full of preposterous nonsense," Alice completed. "I may not have a doctorate, Merida, but I'm not stupid. And if I'm not mistaken, you haven't been too ashamed to stoop to some cheap publicity yourself. 'The exciting new book by the woman who cheated the hangman's noose,' indeed."

"I had nothing to do with the publicity campaign," Merida protested loftily.

"No?" Alice snorted. "Then why did you pose for an author picture with a raven on your shoulder?"

"That was airbrushed in there!" Merida claimed. "Like Oprah's face on Ann-Margret's body."

Too late. Knowing she had scored, Alice stalked past them. "There's nothing up there. I checked. Of course you may see for yourself. I have to go home and cook dinner for my family."

Jackie winced as this shot hit home.

Shivering slightly from the unheated building's damp air, Alice delicately retrieved the surgical scrub gown that Merida had abandoned near the bottom of the staircase (after Maury had accidentally trod on it, nearly causing the paroled murderess to topple backward) and draped it around her shoulders as if it were some queenly wrap. "You better work fast if you want to solve this one, Jackie. I'm way ahead of you, you know."

"This isn't my first time here, Alice," Jackie pointed out.

"Really?" the smug amateur sleuth replied. "I guess not

having as much time to dally around as you single girls,
I'm a little better at getting what I need right off. Yes—
I have one more person to see, Jackie, then I'll be calling
a press conference to name the murderer. Toodle-oo."

Alice moved down and Jackie, Merida, and the two dogs
moved up to the landing above. Jake then nudged Maury,
and the two dogs went off to investigate something. Suddenly the door below flew open, powered by a size eleven
brogan.

"Hold yourself right there!" Officer Sanji ordered.

A little stunned by the entrance of the big policeman
and confused by his ungrammatical request, Alice Blue
hesitated.

"What you be doing here, lady?" Sanji demanded.

"I'm taking a look around," Alice answered indignantly.
"It's a free country."

"Not while I'm here," Sanji retorted grimly. "Who is
using his file-the-nail to be picking the lock, this guy?"

"That's not my file," Alice protested, genuinely innocent.
"The door was open when I came here. I locked it when I
came in so something like this wouldn't happen. If someone
picked that door, they did it after I came here."

Sanji elaborately examined Alice's nails, which were of
medium length, nodded significantly, and then parried, "Ah,
if the door was picked, as you say, then how do you explain
the fact that it was locked when I had to kick it in just now?"

It was clear that the uniformed policeman considered his
cross-examining skills equal to any Rumpole of the New
Delhi Bailey.

"Oh, did you actually try the door before smashing it in?"
Alice asked, feigning great surprise. "How unusual for a
Palmer policeman. Of course I didn't hear anything like a,
'Would you open the door please, this is Officer So-and-So
of the Palmer Police.' Too much to expect, I suppose. May-

be some day. In my children's lifetime, perhaps."

"I am Officer Sanji," the policeman reluctantly introduced himself. "Who be you?"

"I am Alice Blue!" the hardware store owner's wife paused for a wave of realization to wash over the policeman's face. When Sanji's countenance remained unwashed, Alice continued. "And as an alumnus of this university, I have every right to stop in and visit if I want to. Certainly as much a right as those two."

Alice waved her arm disdainfully toward the landing.

Sanji looked up. He saw no trace of any living person. He then looked at the staircase. There were a great many stairs to climb if he really wanted to investigate, and Sanji was already tired from having jogged over from the parking lot when he saw the suspicious lights. More than that, his kicking foot was starting to throb a bit. "Never you mind this! You're accompanying with me to the police station. There we will see where your story is true and when it is not."

Crouched as they were up above in the clocktower belfry of the old building, Jackie and Merida barely heard the shrill cries of anger as Alice Blue was carried away.

"Shall we go down now?" Merida asked.

Jackie looked down the long series of winding staircases to the first floor below and fought back a wave of dizzy nausea. "Give it a few minutes," Merida suggested.

Maury then came bounding up with a prize, a squirrel tail, recently removed.

"Oooh." Jackie shuddered.

"Interesting," Merida responded, using her most clinical tone.

"Where did you get that?" Jackie asked her new puppy. "Never mind. Let's go down."

"Wait, Jackie," Merida's left hand clamped down on Jackie's arm. It felt like a steel vise. "I want to ask you something."

"Okay." Jackie slowly straightened up. Although she was chilly as well, she started taking off her white scrub suit robe. If it came to a fight, perhaps Jackie could wave it for help. Or, if Merida had a knife, perhaps Jackie could wrap it around her wrist in a *CopLady* style defensive move (although the dark-haired film instructor wasn't sure how that worked, exactly).

"What would you say," Merida asked sadly, "if I suggested that we just give up? I'll run away somewhere. Change my name. Just get away from this whole sorry mess."

Jackie shook her head. "That seems a little drastic, Merida. I think if Alice is as close to knowing who did it as she thinks she is, then we must be close too. Why don't we just put our heads together and think?"

"Up here?" Merida asked dubiously. "In the cold?"

"No," Jackie replied, decisively. "Let's take a quick look downstairs then go back to my place for a cup of coffee."

"You weren't thinking of making a plate of those delicious homemade cookies we used to have at the communications faculty teas, were you?" Merida asked hopefully.

"I suppose I could," Jackie conceded. "Just this once."

The two women smiled at each other and shared a laugh before starting to descend. Down, down, down, they went, almost joyful now as they watched Jake teach Maury how to slide down stairs on an old piece of linoleum.

Jackie finally stopped for a breather and asked her new friend, "You really did kill Phil Barger, didn't you, Merida?"

The Hispanic Hitchcock critic gave her a cagey wink. "Kill is such a harsh word, Jackie. Let's just say that whatever happened to my illustrious predecessor was more in the way of pest control."

CHAPTER 15

It didn't take Jackie and Merida more than a few moments of discussion to realize that they needed to broaden their investigation a little if they really wanted to find out what had happened to Walter Hopfelt and Con Mitchell.

Within a few hours they had managed to assemble a group of the interested parties, and the various members of the coffee klatch all pitched in to help prepare refreshments. Indeed, as soon as each new person came, they were ordered to divest themselves of coats and sweaters and put to work in Jackie's warm kitchen on the great cookie project. The one exception to this was the acting medical examiner, Lee Humphries, who it was decided (no offense intended of course) would never touch the food at any time.

"Anyway," Dr. Humphries said in concluding her remarks on what the autopsy of the two former policemen had revealed, "the only important thing to remember is that the methods used to kill these people are virtually untraceable."

"Thank you, Dr. Humphries." Jackie smiled, looking up from kneading the cookie dough by hand in a big bowl. "It's so helpful to have us amateurs to have someone like you come along and fill us in."

"Think nothing of it," remarked the exceptionally tall pathologist, sticking out her legs halfway across the

floor. "There isn't a medical examiner in the country
who wouldn't exchange privileged information for a big
stack of homemade cookies."

"And a nice cup of my chicory coffee," Marcella Jacobs
remarked in her distinctive husky voice. "Don't forget that."

Those drinking coffee toasted the attractive, gray-blonde
local TV reporter with their mugs.

Jackie hadn't known what help Marcella would be, if
any, but she had decided to adopt a policy (similar to
that of the old Hollywood movie stars) of giving a story
exclusively to just one source. This way the privileged
leakee would provide her own security against interloping
intruders. In this case it meant that a half dozen of CIN's
(Palmer's "fewer commercials" station) toughest lay-about
union thugs were manning a tight perimeter ring around
Jackie's house.

"I certainly haven't forgotten your chicory coffee,
Marcie. Although I am drinking something stronger . . ."
Dr. Humphries waved a brimming glass full of the same
bourbon that Peter was brushing on the finished cookies.

"Hey, Mom!" Peter blurted out. He wasn't actually talking to his mother, as he demonstrated by addressing the
question head-on to the willowy medical examiner. "Aren't
female medical examiners like really 'in' these days?"

Jackie laughed. "Are they totally, really 'nifty,' do you
mean?"

Lee Humphries joined in the merriment, sloshing her
cookie-sweetening formula everywhere. "Well, I'm just an
acting medical examiner and I know that's not at all fash-
ionable."

"Where is my dear friend Cosmo Gordon?" Merida
asked.

"Still freezing his . . ."

Jake, under the kitchen table, barked sharply, cutting Dr. Humphries off mid-word. The ex–police dog hated profanity.

" . . . *toes* off, all right?" Humphries continued to make a spectacle of herself by sticking her tongue out at the hero canine. "In Saskatoon, or wherever he is. I don't care if he ever comes back, frankly."

"Hey, watch that stuff," Chief Healy ordered, looking up from his rolling pin. "Cosmo Gordon was the best M.E. this town ever had. If he doesn't come back, we're going to miss him. You can be sure of that."

"I'm not surprised," Dr. Humphries said. "What with all the time he used to spend lounging around over at the police station, ignoring his myriad responsibilities as a doctor to an increasingly sick city."

"Hey," the balding homicide chief protested, "don't blame the pollution problems on the city. We just enforce the laws the City Council lets us enforce. And if you do decide to go looking for a councilman to complain about the law enforcement in this town, just look for a guy with a big horse roll of fifties right here on his hip . . ."

Jackie cut off Chief Healy's graphic mime by clearing her throat loudly. "Perhaps, everyone, we should start cutting back on sampling the bourbon . . ."

" . . . and start drinking my coffee!" Marcella exclaimed shrilly. Then, laughing loudly so that there would be some appreciation of her little joke, the newswoman poured everyone another cup of her bitter brackish coffee.

"So the question is," Jackie asked generally, "did the person who killed Walter Hopfelt do so to hush up whatever he knows about the Danielle Sherman murder?"

"No!" Chief Healy bellowed.

"Why not?" Jackie asked at once.

"We know who killed Danielle Sherman," Healy responded.

"Who?" Merida asked in a dangerous voice.

"Mickey Farrow, a.k.a. Timothy Falloes, former City Council President Morton Slake's old bodyguard," Healy replied positively. "It all fits. He kills Matt Dugan. Danielle Sherman was trying to squeal, she meets the same fate. We know he isn't squeamish about killing women. He's serving life without parole now for killing Slake's mistress Leslie 'Bambi' Worden."

"You found the crucial forensic evidence linking him to Bambi Worden, right?" Jackie asked.

"For whatever that's worth," sniffed Merida Green.

"Right," Healy agreed, answering Jackie's question. "We got him cold. Thanks in part to you."

Jake growled.

"And your wonderful dog here too, of course," Healy added quickly.

That was more like it. Jake disliked self-aggrandizement, but didn't like to hear his old colleagues distort the truth.

"But you didn't actually link Farrow to Matt Dugan's death, did you?" Jackie asked.

"Well," Healy replied, miserably fingering the edge of a partially flattened length of dough. "No, we didn't. We didn't have to after he went down on the Worden charge. But it makes sense that he did the killing, doesn't it?"

"If you look at it a certain way," Jackie agreed. "But that's not the only way to approach this question."

Jackie dropped her left hand to her side as she used her right hand to scratch the side of her nose.

Maury immediately began to lick the dough off her fingers.

"Maury!" Jackie exclaimed. Giving the others a "What are you going to do?" look, she walked over to the sink to wash her hands.

Just then, there was a loud thump on her back door. Signalling Peter that it was okay, Jackie let her son open it.

A big, whale-bellied man with a black mourning band on his sleeve (in honor of the former Local 72 legend, the late Spike Fitzgerald) and a faraway look on his face, said, "Excuse me, Ms. Jacobs."

"What is it, Mashie?" Marcella asked quickly.

"There's a lady tried to get through." The union laborer stifled a belch before continuing. "Real pushy. We had to push her. To get her away, y'know? She won't come back again. Not if she knows what's good for her."

"Thanks, Mashie," Marcella beamed, showing the technician a little leg to keep him interested. "Keep up the good work."

"Wait a minute," Jackie said, before Peter could slam the door shut again. "Excuse me . . . sir!"

The big stagehand, nicknamed for his favorite way to prepare potatoes, quickly turned back. "Mashie's fine. Say, some of those cookies wouldn't happen to be for us, would they?"

"We'll bring some out as soon as they're done," Jackie promised, ignoring the groans of those who now pictured endless additional hours of cookie making in a futile attempt to fill the gaping maws of the burly union men. "About that woman?"

"She's history!"

"I'm sure she is," Jackie responded, feeling her eyes water from the stagehand's beer and onion breath.

"Took off—towards the college, it looked like."

"Oh well," Jackie replied, trying to sound philosophical. "What did she look like, incidentally?"

Mashie shrugged and adopted his handicapper's face. "Aaah—maybe a six. Six point five. Something like that. Short, but curvy. Legs good. Top okay. She don't start losing points till you get to the mug, then it's downhill on one ski time."

"Her face was broken out, like with a bad case of acne," Jackie guessed.

"Like she lost an acid fight," the big man confirmed.

"Great, thanks," Jackie responded. "You want to lick the batter bowls?"

"Is the pope Polish?" Then, grabbing the bowl as if it were a football, Mashie rushed back outside.

"Marcella . . ." Jackie said.

"What?" the much-put-upon newswoman shrieked. She had been drinking strong coffee and making circles of dough with a small cup for what seemed like hours and her temper was short.

"Didn't you tell your men I have a duplex neighbor who might need to get in?" Jackie asked indignantly.

"Are you talking about Wackadoodle Dugan?" Marcella asked disdainfully. "I thought she stayed in her apartment all the time ordering in and driving you crazy?"

"Marcella!" Jackie exclaimed. "That's not the point. She does live here. If she wants to go out, she can. Maybe she's working these days."

"She is," Healy confirmed. "In the park. She sells jewelry in one of those little booths."

Jackie gave Healy a curious look. "Jewelry? In Beakins Park? By the monument? By the guy who sells lemon ices? That area?"

Healy nodded.

"Are you sure?"

"Positive." Healy nodded. "She's still on parole, you know. I've seen her jacket. She's got to report where she's living and where she's working or back in the clink she goes."

"Fascists," Merida muttered under her breath.

"Hey, what did you say?"

"Nothing, nothing."

Jackie grabbed Healy's forearm. "Chief, never mind. What was Xenia in jail for?"

"Well," Healy answered, "she never really served any time in jail. She got her arresting officer to marry her and then of course he couldn't testify."

"What did she do?" Jackie repeated.

"Shoplift. A sticky fingers," Healy further explained, employing a graphic mime. "It was like a sickness with her. She'd get busted. Bail herself out and go right back to the store. No one wanted to put her in jail because of the two kids. They were babies in those days."

"So those children aren't Matt's?" Jackie asked.

"No," Healy responded derisively. "You know old softy Dugan. He loved kids. Probably treated them like they were his own. But those little girls came with the package. That's what tore him up so much. He managed to keep his wife under control for a while, but then she started up again. He tried to keep a lid on it, hauling stuff back to the store, paying for what they couldn't return. Anything to keep those two kids from losing their mother. Crazy witch. Excuse my language, but you don't understand what it's like to see a good policeman ground down to pulp before your eyes. He got on the bottle and couldn't get off. That's when he started to go after the mayor."

"Jane Bellamy?" Merida asked.

"Big Bill Curtis," Jackie corrected her. "He was the father, wasn't he? Of Xenia's two girls."

Healy's eyes bugged slightly. "How did you know that? McGowan tell you?"

"No, you just did." Jackie smiled. "Actually, it makes sense now. It certainly explains the kid-glove, red-carpet treatment Xenia's gotten after Matt Dugan died."

Healy rubbed his face roughly. "Yeah, well. I'll tell you, people may have felt sorry for her at first, but she blew that pretty quick."

"And how!" hooted the now slightly more sober acting medical examiner. "You should have heard Cosmo go on about the widow and children of his dear chum Matt Dugan before they actually met. 'Oh, the poor woman! What can we do for her? Oh the poor wee bairns.' "

"Ah, then Dr. Gordon is Scots, is he?" Frances asked with interest. Murderers frankly never interested the elderly former telephone operator nearly as much as a person's ethnic heritage.

"Western Canadian, which is almost as bad," Lee Humphries responded. "And then Cosmo had Xenia Dugan and her little terrors over and you never again heard a word about poor Matt Dugan. Except once—when he was coming out of his office and didn't know anybody was listening, I heard him say, 'You're well out of it, Matt Dugan, not to have to spend another moment with that woman . . . ' "

Peter led those who knew Cosmo Gordon in a wave of laughter for Dr. Humphries's uncanny impersonation. Jackie couldn't afford the laugh, however. She was beginning to put things together. Suppose someone had a reason to kill Matt Dugan and Danielle Sherman for reasons other than that they might be links in a chain of secrets about shady dealings in City Hall.

Chief Healy put down his rolling pin and empty glass and stood unsteadily up. "Well, there's just one way to find out. Talk to the man."

"That's what I was about to suggest," Jackie began.

"We're gonna drive over," Healy announced. "You and me, and of course Felix and the dog over there, if he wants to come, and have us a little talk with Big Bill Curtis."

"But, Chief," Jackie protested. "I know . . ."

"No, ma'am," Healy said firmly. "With all due respect, you don't know. You have an idea and you can tell me what it is on the way over. Then maybe I'll come up with a few ideas, and with me being on the homicide beat myself for about eighteen years, maybe my ideas will be a little better . . ."

"Hey!" Peter interrupted. "Don't be insulting my mother! You guys couldn't find a skateboard on Oak Street!"

Healy smarted at the insult—Oak Street was famous for its highly competitive skate-offs.

"He's right, you know," cackled Lee Humphries.

Healy rubbed his hand down his face and his thinning scalp turned bright crimson in irritation. "I'm taking Ms. Walsh here over to Big Bill Curtis's to assist me in my investigation of a very serious murder and I don't want to hear another word about it!"

"But she's telling you, Chief," Merida called out, "that she may know who did it and going to Curtis won't help."

"Well, she's been wrong before," Healy snapped. "Look at you. You're out on the street and the department had to put up with months of abuse for arresting the wrong woman before that. From now on, I'm going to make dead sure I got the right person. I'll get a confession—on video tape—if I have to beat it out of 'em the old-fashioned way."

As Jackie was escorted forcibly to the car by Healy and his partner Felix Cruz, the others looked on slackjawed.

At length, Frances commented, "Well, if Jackie and the policeman aren't going to be here, we might as well call it quits with the cookies."

"Omigod!" cried Peter. "What are we going to do?"

"I think I'm going to go lie down," moaned Dr. Humphries, walking unsteadily toward the living room sofa.

"And I'm going after them," announced Merida calmly.

"But you don't have a car," Marcella pointed out.

Merida turned to Frances. "Mrs. Costello, I'd like your permission to borrow Jackie's Jeep."

"Oh, dear."

"I'm not going to hurt it," Merida promised. "I'm just going to follow them. Believe me, and I speak from experience, if the police know you have someone outside waiting and watching and making a little bit of noise about letting them go, things move a lot quicker."

"So you'll go after her in her car?"

Merida nodded. "And wait outside and this way she'll have transportation without begging them to drive her home in the police car."

Frances clearly was on the verge of saying yes. "Are you . . . ?"

"A wonderful driver?" Merida replied deadpan. "All poisoners are wonderful drivers. Read your Colin Wilson—*Criminal History of Mankind*."

"Will you be safe?" Frances asked.

Merida nodded. "If you let me go now, so I don't have to race frantically after them."

"All right, then," Frances decided. "God bless. The Jeep, I mean. I hope to Providence she's got enough insurance."

Merida wiped off her hands. "Peter, find your mother's spare keys. Don't dally. You heard what the chief said about beating up people to get answers."

Peter gulped and rushed off.

"And bring in my jacket from the hall closet," Merida called after him. "The black leather one! It makes me look like Mercedes McCambridge," she confided to the others, "but it's warm and I lost my good coat in the explosion at Con's house."

Merida then turned to the television journalist on the high stool. "Marcella, can you ask your men if anyone followed them?"

Marcella considered a moment, then responded, "I'm sure someone did. And I'm sure they'll call me . . ." The tele-journalist indicated with a sweep of her hand the cellular phone hanging out of her handbag. " . . . when they get to where they're going. The problem is . . ."

Merida nodded for Marcella to continue as Peter returned to the room with the keys and her leather jacket. Before he could move away, Merida grabbed him by the sleeve and gestured for him not to leave.

"We don't have any right to be there," Marcella resumed. "The courts are getting very picky about newsteams following the police around on a hunch that they might do something newsworthy. They claim that we're hindering law enforcement. Especially when we show the police questioning a judge about taking a bribe."

"Well, then you can cover me," Merida offered. "I'm newsworthy, right? So you can say you're working on a story. 'Palmer's most notorious paroled murderer pursued the city's most famous amateur sleuth to a midnight conclave with an exiled political boss earlier this evening . . . ' "

"I like it," Marcella beamed. "That's very good, you know."

"I am a writer," Merida responded. "And I've spent a lot of time the last two years watching television. Come on, Peter. You're coming too."

"I am?"

"I'll need you to help with the dogs."

Frances emitted a troubled, "Oh . . ."

"I'm very good with them," Merida advised Jackie's worried mother. "I've lived with a dog handler, you know."

"Yes, well," Frances protested. "You'll find those two brutes are a lot more difficult than a couple of stuffed ones."

Merida grimaced. "Oh, you heard about that one, did you? Well, Con did have his strange little peccadilloes. Still, I miss him. Come on."

Peter stood for a moment, his hands in his pockets. "I'm a little scared."

Merida smiled. "So am I. You'll get over it as long as you can concentrate real hard on what you're doing." Merida then turned to Marcella. "I'll need to be in touch with you so I know where I'm driving. May I borrow your cellular phone? You can use the house phone to coordinate."

"No, sorry," Marcella answered. "This phone costs almost ten thousand dollars. It has three lines and the folks in the field aren't going to know to call me at this number. Doesn't Jackie have a car phone?"

Peter shook his head.

Marcella was amazed. "No phone? I know she doesn't have a car radio. How does she find out what the traffic is?"

"She looks out the window," Frances snapped. "And before you ask, no I don't have a car phone in my old heap, either. I don't know where you're going to get your hands on one."

"I do," Peter offered quickly.

"Where?"

Even Jake, who had reluctantly returned to the kitchen at Jackie's order, wanted to know the answer to that one.

"Doc Humphries has one," Peter replied, nodding toward the woman who was now fast asleep on the couch. "In her coat. I saw it when she came in."

The three women looked at him and together gave him an "Isn't that cute?" smile.

"He is twelve years old," Frances pointed out. "Ah, Lord love us. In another three or four years we'll all be worrying that he's fathering broods of children. Not that there's anything wrong, mind you, with large families. JP and meself were so disappointed when Jackie couldn't give us a wee little granddaughter . . ."

"I'll get Maury and wait outside." Peter sulked. "C'mon, Jake."

Merida turned to Marcella. "Marcy, could I ask you to find the phone and program the number into your phone?"

"Okay," Marcella responded, as if doing the older woman a tremendous favor. Actually, she was anxious to get her hands on the device. If she got the assistant medical examiner's number, phone make, and model number, the boys and girls in the lab of the network's parent company could figure out a way to tap the phone at will.

As the tall gray-blond reporter left the room, Merida approached Frances. "All right, Mrs. Costello . . ."

"Please. *Frances.*"

"Frances, of course." Merida smiled—always an unsettling event. "If the doctor wakes up, tell her we borrowed her phone. Also see if she ever found out—or can find out—if the heroin found injected into Danielle Sherman could possibly be matched with confiscated drugs from the police property room. Ask her to check the property records of both the central and university precincts. Most of the principals in this case bounced back and forth. Think you can remember all that?"

"I think I can hold that much on me brain for a few moments." The retired telephone operator then gave Merida a shrewd look. "What does all this mean, Merry? That one of the policemen killed her? Your policeman, for instance?"

"Close," Merida confessed. "But not my policeman. Or Walter Hopfelt either. If they had, they wouldn't have been killed to cover someone else's trail. Besides, those two weren't killers. But they might have been persuaded to steal some heroin from the property stores. Especially if they didn't know why the person wanted it."

Frances raised her orange-dyed eyebrows in mock surprise. "Would it have been that easy, now?"

Merida nodded emphatically. "From what I hear, Frances, when that fellow Woltzer—you know, the one that was in the paper for being beaten up for not paying his bookies—ran things, you could have had anything you wanted, for a price."

"Well, go if you're going," Frances responded. The older woman was obviously upset to be hearing about such blatant police corruption when her only daughter was in their clutches.

Merida sensed this and touched her arm with strong, reassuring fingers. "Don't worry, Frances. I'll make sure she's okay."

And so, without another word, the convicted murderess rushed off to save Jackie Walsh from the police.

CHAPTER 16

The home Jackie and Cooper Walsh had lived in during their eleven years together had changed quite a bit. Liz Curtis, Cooper's mostly live-in girlfriend these days (although she kept her own small apartment to go back to on the weekends when Peter visited), had completely redecorated.

Jackie realized now, in the wisdom of her years, that their early, somewhat tongue-in-cheek decision to go for the gilt and chintz look of *Sunset Boulevard* had been rather silly. Of course she and Cooper had more or less abandoned that style after Peter was born and who proved to be quite the little furniture destroyer. Then, over the years, they had replaced the items one by one with whatever was on sale. The furniture had been sturdy and comfortable, but it certainly hadn't ever impressed anyone into taking a picture of it.

The Liz Curtis makeover, with oversized furniture covered with Laura Ashley prints, had been featured in two Sunday supplements and the area edition of *EH* (an unfortunate shortening of its original name *Elegant Homes*, done in order to appeal to a more eclectic readership).

Had this interview/interrogation been conducted at the Curtis mansion, Jackie might have put up more of a fight to stay in the police car. However, when the former mayor insisted on moving the meet to his ex-wife's house to avoid the reporters, of course Jackie had to see what the woman had done with the decor.

"Are you paying attention, Ms. Walsh?" the red-faced Chief Healy demanded of her.

Jackie, who of course had not been listening, glibly replied, "No. Actually, I'm a little light-headed from having my blood circulation being cut off by these cuffs. I could sue, you know." Healy had slipped the cuffs on her after she'd tried to jump out of the car at an intersection on the way over.

Healy gave her a look, then gestured for Cruz to unlock them.

Big Bill Curtis, a broad-chested, red-haired ex-marine with a bushy handlebar mustache, took advantage of the opportunity to attack. "What the hell is going on here, Healy? You drag me out of the house in the middle of the night for some questions. Then I come here and you've got some frizzy-haired person already under arrest. What the hell then was the point of bothering *me*? I can't identify her, and you certainly could have waited for a more convenient time if that's all we're here for."

"No, sir."

"Is she the guilty party, yes or no? And if the answer is yes, then what the hell do you need with us?" Curtis's broad arm sweep also indicated his ex-wife Elizabeth McKean Curtis, younger sister of Phyllis McKean Greenaway, the wife of the former police commissioner.

Liz Curtis was a large-boned, high-cheekboned, basically intelligent woman with a halo of shimmering gray-white hair. She kept her hand placed protectively on the knee of Cooper Walsh, a thin, athletic, gray-bearded salesman who had been Jackie's first high school sweetheart, then later, the kind, caring young man who had helped her get over the loss of her beloved Pryor Kincaid (when the latter had died in a boating accident somewhere off Puerto Vallarta).

Neither of them rose to second Big Bill's opinion. They knew that Jackie was in their home as a sleuth, not a suspect, and wanted to see how the game would be played out.

Jackie, now free, immediately got to her feet. "May I use the bathroom?"

"Of course," Liz responded. She started to give directions, but Jackie cut her off.

"I lived here ten years, I think I still remember the way. Oh, don't get up, Cooper."

Walsh, who clearly hadn't intended to do so, simmered a moment and then took out his wrath on Healy. "Big Bill is right, Chief. What's the purpose of this masquerade? My girlfriend and I didn't even know Walter Hopfelt."

"Actually you may have met him at the university when you were married to Jackie, dear," Liz pointed out.

"Met him?" Cooper sputtered. "For what, five minutes? Had a conversation with him about the best place to park the car? Give me a break!"

"Apparently once you serve in public office, Cooper," Big Bill explained, "they have a right to take shots at you forever. You really should leave Cooper out of this though, Chief. Whatever you may think of me and my associates, none of it has anything to do with this gentleman."

"Thank you!" Walsh said loudly.

Liz then squeezed his knee, telling him to hush.

Healy turned angrily to the former mayor of the city. "I didn't bring him into this, Curtis. You did, by insisting on meeting here. I told Walsh when I came in and I'll tell him again now, he's not the focus of this investigation and can leave at any time." Healy then turned to Cooper. "Is that clear, sir? Do you want to leave?"

"No," Walsh said at once.

"Then how about making yourself useful by getting us all some coffee?"

Jackie turned up the taps to full, not to drown out the squawks from her outraged former husband, but to try to cover the sound of the creaky bathroom window as she hammered on it with a big plastic brush in an ineffectual attempt to open it. After a moment, there was a tap on the door and Jackie realized that Felix Cruz, the emaciated Dominican detective, must be standing just outside the door. "You alright in there?"

"Just trying to rub away the deep red marks on my wrists, Sergeant," Jackie yelled in response. She then decided that what she was about to attempt was ridiculous. It would be a tight fit, and she would come down outside in a dense growth of shrubs. If Jackie didn't break a leg, she would still have to make her way through the dark streets of Kingswood to her home twenty miles away without being seen. Talk about impossible escapes!

Giving up the idea, Jackie washed her face, fixed her makeup, and re-emerged in the living room in time to see Liz Curtis put down a tray of coffee and a small plate of cookies and to hear Big Bill exclaim, "What do you mean this really has to do with the killing of Matt Dugan? If that doesn't beat the band with a hammer. I tell you— I am sick to death about hearing sob stories about some sozzlehead who couldn't even keep a job with the Palmer Police Department!"

"This is also about your daughter, Big Bill," Jackie responded.

"Great!" Curtis growled. "Now I'm on a first-name basis with murderers. You care to expand on that, lady?"

"First of all," Jackie responded. "I'm not a murderer. And if I was, I would certainly not be the first murderer you chose to associate with. Not by a long shot."

"Touché, William," Liz commented, snapping off a bite of an icebox cookie.

Healy, afraid he wouldn't get any, all but sprinted over to the sideboard to fill his hands and pockets.

"You keep your damn mouth shut!" Curtis raged at his ex-wife. "Remember our divorce agreement. You flap your gums and you'll never see another dime from me as long as you live."

Liz made a zipping motion across her lips.

"I mean, Mayor Curtis," Jackie continued, "that we think that the same person killed your daughter, Matt Dugan, Walter Hopfelt, and probably Con Mitchell."

"Give me a break!" Curtis bawled derisively. "Try to have empathy for someone besides yourself. We lost our child. It still hurts. Even after two years. It will hurt us the rest of our life."

Liz used a crumb-bestrewn napkin to stifle a sudden sob.

"First we heard that she killed herself," Curtis continued. "Then that Merida Green killed her—then that she was murdered and raped by some biker, and now every month or so, whenever the papers have a slow day they drag out some new crackpot theory. Everyone from Bluebeard to Martians to the ghost of that damn lecher Philip Barger has been held responsible. I don't find it funny. I don't find it useful. And I consider it a damn shame that my baby, much as I loved her, can't rest easy in her grave without a bunch of graveside ravens trying to pull up some of her bones." Curtis was really getting worked up now and Cruz started fingering his service weapon in case he had to kneecap the former mayor.

"It was a botched investigation! It was a botched autopsy and I'll be damned if I'm going to stand still and watch nit-wits issue irresponsible statements to the press that you've now decided that my daughter was the victim of some serial killer!" Curtis finished.

"We're not saying that, sir," Jackie argued.

Healy quickly cut the dark-haired film instructor off. "Serial killer, huh?" Visions of collaborating with the FBI and having someone ghostwrite a best-selling true crime book with his name on it raged through Healy's sugar-fueled brain like wildfire. "You know, I hadn't thought of that angle. It fits though, if you think about it for a minute."

Curtis, knowing exactly where the chief of detectives was coming from, snarled, "Then if you think about it for *two* minutes, Healy, it falls apart into goulash. My daughter and those three men had nothing in common. They were killed at different times and in different ways. It's not that big a town, they may have all known each other, but obviously I didn't involve my daughter in my political dealings. And I certainly wouldn't have let any of those cops near any major investigation."

"What about . . . ?" Jackie started.

"What?" Curtis raged. "What crackpot notion are you going to insult our intelligence with this time?"

"I wonder," Jackie continued coolly, "if maybe whoever killed Danielle did it because he thought she was cheating on him? With Matt Dugan and with Con Mitchell . . ."

"Not with Walter Hopfelt surely," Liz Curtis interjected.

"No, I think perhaps Hopfelt was blackmailing him."

"Him?" Healy questioned sharply. "I thought you were convinced that it was a woman."

"Convinced?" Jackie assumed an innocent look. "I didn't say I was convinced, Chief. Who am I to be convinced of anything when it comes to crime solving? After all, I'm just a wooly headed academic who teaches a film course."

"Oh brother," Walsh responded quietly. He, if no one else, saw the trap being primed.

Big Bill jumped back in, for the first time sincerely interested. "You're talking about that dweeb Surtees, aren't you?"

"Think about it," Jackie said quickly. "When you first investigated the Barger murder, Chief Healy, who had the most plausible means, method, motive, and opportunity?"

"Well, the Surtees kid, I guess," Healy confessed. "He was the only one strong enough to drag Barger from his office to the editing suite where you found him."

"Philip Barger wasn't that heavy," Jackie pointed out. "But, yes. David Surtees could have done it very easily. Go on."

Healy hated to abandon the lucrative serial killer theory, but answered nonetheless, "Surtees had an editing room key."

"And," Jackie added, "David was one of the few people Barger occasionally trusted with a key to his office. He and David were working on the credit sequence of the Kestral trilogy miniseries when Philip died. David could have easily copied the key and then used it to get in to doctor the booze."

"Then after he killed Barger for seducing my daughter, he killed her too?" Curtis proposed.

Jackie nodded. "Either as part of his plan or perhaps when she threatened to turn him in. Whether she had proof he did it or not, David would have been the first one Danielle suspected."

"Of course!" Curtis raged. "How could I have been so blind and not seen this before? I never liked that pencil-necked little geek."

Jackie gave a quick private smile. She had strongly suspected as much.

"What about that policeman?" Liz Curtis asked.

"Who, me?" asked Healy.

"No, the dead policeman."

"Which one?" Healy rasped. "There are three of them, remember?"

"The red-headed one," Liz said impatiently. "Uh, what was his name? You know the one I mean, Bill—the bagman who used to meet with you . . ."

"What the hell!" Curtis's face turned bright scarlet at the casual admission of his criminal past.

"I'm sorry," Liz responded. "It's late. I'm tired and frankly a little upset at all this talk that Danielle's young man could have been the one who murdered her."

"Don't worry, Ms. Curtis," Healy rushed to assure her. "We'll all pretend we didn't hear a word."

"Yeah, you'll pretend today," Big Bill predicted. "And six months from now you'll be coming around with your hand out."

Jackie headed off the argument with a quick, "In answer to your question, Liz—Matt Dugan, your husband's so-called bagman and Danielle did meet several times. David knew about that, but may not have known why. He may have thought Dugan was a rival. We thought for a while that Matt Dugan was grilling Danielle on the affairs of your husband. Perhaps David Surtees was worried that they were discussing him."

"And Con Mitchell?" Healy asked.

"Same motives," Jackie replied. "Con met Danielle at the old Blue Jay the night she was found dead. Surtees could have thought he was another rival . . ."

Healy nodded to himself. "Mitchell did have a reputation for being a ladies' man."

"And Surtees could have thought Dani was turning him into the police," Liz supplied. "He killed my daughter and then paid off the policeman."

Jackie shook her head. "No, I don't think Mitchell was that kind of cop. Do you, Chief?"

Healy took a moment, then shook his head as well. "Mitchell was a jerk in a lot of ways but I never heard he took."

"Anyone will take if you make the right offer," Curtis snarled. "Especially a policeman."

Jackie again intervened to head off an argument between the gruff Irish homicide chief of detectives and the cynical former mayor. "I don't think Con Mitchell knew that it was David. He had to break off his relationship with Merida when she became a suspect in the Philip Barger murder. It's possible that Con Mitchell believed what most people believed, that Merida killed Danielle to cover up whatever she knew about that killing. But then she was paroled recently and managed to convince all of us that she hadn't done the second killing."

"So Mitchell knew it had to be the geek," Curtis finished.

Jackie nodded as if she agreed. "Somehow Walter Hopfelt got in the middle. We know from his association with Stewart Goodwillie that he was definitely not above taking bribes."

"Surtees killed Hopfelt for blackmailing him?" Healy asked. "Then this must have been going on for several years."

"David has been taking a punishing amount of outside work recently," Jackie informed the others, "including the Olympics. Which is odd when we all know he hates sports."

Healy nodded. It was all coming together. It would have been better if it was a serial killer, but on the other hand,

the Police Guild's representative had been telling people
that the whole serial killer thing was getting to be old
hat and these days Hollywood was looking for just plain
good old-fashioned crimes of passion killings so there was
a possibility he could still clean up. Hell, if that girl in New
York rated three separate movies, an even prettier girl in
Palmer should at least be good for some cable network
schlock exploitation movie of the week.

"So maybe," the chief contributed, "Surtees got tired of
paying."

"I used my influence," Jackie continued, "with Stewart
Goodwillie . . ."

The others didn't have to be reminded that Jackie had
been involved in numerous run-ins with Palmer's richest
man, a noted inventor and pharmacological tycoon who
had recently abandoned his other pursuits to run a highly
successful bottled water business.

" . . . to talk to Evan Stillman," Jackie continued.

"Stillman!"

Having intentionally brought up the name to aggravate
Healy, Jackie now pretended to calm him down. "I know,
Chief. He got you fired and almost became police commis-
sioner . . ."

" . . . before a new broom swept all of us old boys out,"
Curtis finished.

"Anyway," Jackie resumed, "former Acting Commissioner Stillman now works for Mr. Goodwillie as his new
head of security."

"I know Stillman," Cooper interjected. "He's a good
man. Got an eight handicap over at Hawks Crest and that's
not an easy course."

Jackie grimaced, recalling that her ex-husband could never believe anything could be amiss with a fellow golfer.
"Former Captain Stillman told me that since he has taken

over, he'd ended the financial arrangement with Hopfelt. What was it you told me earlier tonight, Chief? About . . . ?

" . . . Walter Hopfelt leading the good life?" Healy anticipated. "Yeah. No doubt about it. Hopfelt loved to spend money, between his gourmet restaurant meals and his quarter-of-a-million-dollar personal computer virtual reality system, Walter was always on the lookout for a supplementary buck."

Curtis went to the corner bar and poured himself a stiff shot and downed it.

"My God," the former mayor said hoarsely, wiping his mouth with the back of his hand, "it fits like a pair of Zug Snug gloves, doesn't it?"

Jackie continued, apparently almost unnecessarily, "Walter Hopfelt was killed the week Merida was released from prison. Con Mitchell the week Merida moved in with him."

Liz Curtis looked up from her crocheting to comment, "He saw that one of his murders had been unofficially blamed on Merida Green and figured, why not frame her for two more crimes as well?"

"Why not indeed?" Jackie remarked. And then with a new angry tone to her voice, she related, "And do you know what makes me mad? That he tried to use us, me especially, to reopen the Danielle Sherman case. If Merida could have been found guilty of that murder, we would have assumed her guilty, without bothering to have a trial, that she killed Walter Hopfelt and Con Mitchell too."

"Brilliant." Curtis groaned. "If I had a thinker like that on my staff, I'd still be mayor. Hell, governor. Hell, president."

All of a sudden, the free-wheeling discussion was interrupted by the entrance of two barking dogs.

"Jake!" Jackie cried out. "Maury!"

Jake immediately bounded to Jackie's side, collected a

quick hug, then took up a defensive position.

Maury tried to do the same, but instead, slipped on the polished wood foyer floor and crashed noisily into a fragile table with vase, smashing it to pieces.

"Good dog," Jackie muttered under her breath.

Merida Green then appeared in the doorway with the brilliant, bald, bespectacled solicitor of Rodgers University, Silas Herring.

"Merida!" Jackie called out.

"Jackie!" she called back. "Are you all right?"

"Chief of Detectives Lorne Healy," Herring boomed in his surprising cello voice, "I have here a writ of habeas corpus."

Healy immediately threw up his hands in supplication. "Lawyer Herring, I wouldn't dream of holding your client. In fact, we're just about to take a little trip across town to make an arrest. Anyone who's coming, grab your coats. Felix!"

The detective sergeant, who had been pushed aside as if a silly nuisance, stuck his head a little farther into the room. "Yes, Chief?"

"Get the vehicle warmed up. Get the address of Surtees, first name David. Any middle initial?" Healy asked, turning to the others.

There were no responses. Finally Jackie turned to Jake. "Jake, you know David Surtees, from the university. Does he have a middle name?"

The big dog thought for a moment and then barked twice for no.

"That's amazing," Merida remarked, echoing the thoughts of many in the room.

"Thank you," Healy responded. He then turned back to Felix. "And call the precinct. Tell 'em to seal off his street."

"Yes, sir!" Cruz yelled, narrowly avoiding tripping over

Maury in his haste to exit. Confusion abounded, and Jackie slipped quietly out of the room.

Healy grabbed his hat and announced, "I'm leaving to make an arrest. If you all want to tag along, you may. Just stay out of my way."

As Healy exited hurriedly, Big Bill Curtis regarded Peter and Merida with befuddlement and asked them, "How did you get in here?"

Peter held out his hand. "I have a key."

Jackie, returning to the room, rushed to her son and held his arms. "Peter, you stay here."

"But, Mom! Didn't I just save you?"

Jackie smiled. "Yes, you did, darling. And you did a magnificent job. But now I have to know that you are out of harm's way. So I can do my job."

Peter looked deep into his mother's eyes. "What do you want me to do, Mom?"

"Stay here with your father." Jackie turned to her husband. "You're going to be here, aren't you, Coop?"

He nodded.

Jackie kissed Peter on the area above his upper lip. There were thin, silky hairs there now. "Are you growing a mustache, Peter?"

The adolescent boy giggled, then after another brief hug, mother and son parted. Closer than ever before.

CHAPTER 17

David Surtees's apartment house was a prewar building with a white aluminum-sided exterior. The homicide detectives Healy and Cruz were the first to arrive at the Faneuil Hall Apartments. They were allowed entrance by the doorman and then pressed the bell for the elevator. Before the achingly slow elevator finally arrived, they were joined by Big Bill Curtis (who had followed the plain-clothes police car in his own vehicle), Jackie and Merida (who had arrived at the apartment building a distant third in Jackie's red Jeep), Marcella Jacobs and her television crew (who had been summoned by cellular phone by Merida on the way over), and Alice Blue (who had been stalking them all in her little Honda Civic).

There would have been a terrific argument, in all likelihood, but then the elevator doors opened. Not everyone could fit, so Healy left behind Jackie, her two dogs, Alice Blue, and Detective Felix Cruz.

While Alice ranted, and the chief ascended in the elevator in the exclusive company of a murderer and a TV news team—Jackie, Jake, Maury, and Felix climbed the stairs.

"Any chance that that big dog of yours has a keg of beer around his neck?" Cruz asked Jackie.

"You should be ashamed of yourself," Jackie panted,

going along with the joke. "He's not old enough to carry a keg yet, he's still a puppy."

At this point Cruz croaked out, "I'd settle for a mug."

By the time they reached Surtees's apartment, the door was open and they could walk right in. Deciding which way to go was easy enough, the L-shaped layout forced them left. A quick look into each high-ceilinged plant-bestrewn room, yielded no signs of human life. It wasn't until they reached the end of the hall that they found a mass of people milling around the door to Surtees's bathroom.

The young film editor, trying desperately to cover himself with a wash cloth and to shield his date with his own body, blinked in the harsh glare of KCIN's mobile news camera.

"David Surtees!" Healy yelled, standing in front of the monitor the editing instructor had hooked up in the bathroom so he could watch appropriate videos while bathing. "We'd like you to towel off and . . ."

"What is this?" Surtees sputtered. "What are you people doing here? How did you get in?"

"I knocked on the door," Healy replied. "You shouted, 'Come in . . . ' "

"That was the girl in the video," Surtees protested.

Healy turned around, blinded in the glare, and then turned off the monitor. He then turned back to the two hot-tubbers. "Be that as it may, I'm in and if I made a mistake, it was an honest one, fully sanctioned by the Supreme Court. So don't expect to get off on a technicality."

"Getting off is the least of my problems right now," Surtees responded.

A voice was then heard from behind the exposed editor. "David! Who is it?"

Surtees did not answer his date, instead addressing his questions to the chief of detectives. "Am I under arrest?"

"Bingo!" tersed Healy.

"For what?"

"You're a suspect in the murder of Walter Hopfelt."

"Me?"

"No, David," Jackie responded. "You, Xenia."

Xenia Dugan, Jackie's duplex neighbor slithered out from behind Surtees, not caring what she revealed.

"Is that you, Jackie?"

"Yes, Xenia. Would you like a towel and your glasses?"

"Wait a minute!" Surtees exclaimed. "You're saying Xenia's involved with Walter Hopfelt's death?"

"She lured him to a room in the Sabin Hughes Annex, then startled him into breaking his neck," Jackie responded.

"Why for God's sake?" Surtees cried wildly.

"You know why, Xenia," Jackie directed her comments to the splashing former Mrs. Dugan. "You killed Matt, didn't you? Out of jealousy. You thought he was having an affair with Danielle Sherman?"

"While I was pregnant with his baby!" Xenia wailed. "I fixed him, though. After I killed him, I got an abortion!"

While the others in the room winced, Jackie continued her accusations. "Then Walter Hopfelt had to be disposed of for blackmailing you."

"Well, blackmailing is against the law, isn't it?" Xenia did her best, in spite of the circumstances, to seem sententious. "I knew nobody would listen to me. Just because I've had my own troubles with the law, no one cares what people do to me. It's like saying a streetwalker can't be raped."

"How long was Hopfelt blackmailing you?" Jackie asked somewhat sympathetically.

"I don't know. Two years. Then he wanted more money than we agreed on." Xenia's voice immediately became shrill. "Where was I supposed to get it? He was already bleeding me dry! I only meant to scare him. It was an accident!"

"And Con Mitchell?"

Xenia's entire body seemed to blush.

Marcella signalled her cameraman to turn up the red spectrum on his instruments.

Merida Green, who had elbowed her way in, pinned Xenia with an accusation. "You had an affair with him? Didn't you? While I was in jail. I found little bits of underclothes around. Flimsy little things like these." Merida held up Xenia's teddy which had been lying on the floor. "And that charm bracelet with those X's—did you realize you'd left that behind?"

Jackie gasped. Xenia grabbed the garment out of Merida's hand and pressed it to her body, covering herself the best she could. "No! You're a liar. And Con didn't love you. He loved me. He was going to tell you. He promised me!"

"Before or after you blew him up, Xenia?" Jackie asked.

"Go ahead, and tell her," Alice Blue yelled. "She bought some lye and some concentrated paraffin oil from my husband's hardware store. He warned her that if they got mixed, it would make a helluva bomb. I thought she got it for her boyfriend here . . ."

"No," Jackie responded. "I let the chief and Bill Curtis think so too so they would come over here. When I figured it out, I made a quick call to Xenia from my house . . . I mean, Cooper's house. No answer. But when I called here, you picked up, Xenia. I had a feeling you two would hit it off.

"It was Xenia all along," Jackie continued. "I should have suspected her a long time ago. It's just that she acted so stupid most of the time, I didn't realize it was an act."

Xenia's eyes flashed with long-suppressed hate. "You think you're so smart, don't you, Miss Movies? You never suspected how I wheedled my way into your building so I could keep an eye on you. The great detective. All those killings and she never suspected her own neighbor."

"No, Xenia," Jackie confessed. "You claimed you were helpless so many times I would have never thought you capable of carrying out all those murders all by yourself."

"By myself!" Xenia blazed. "Yes, that's the problem, isn't it? Nobody ever stands up for me. I have to do everything myself. Look at you!" Xenia exclaimed, pushing Surtees. "Why don't you say something to these people. Do you want to see me go to jail?"

Surtees gave the distraught widow a look. "If you really killed those people? Sure. I absolutely want to see you in jail if you're guilty of murder."

"I hate you!" Xenia lashed out, pushing Surtees out of the tub. "You're just like them. Men! You're no good! You're just no good!" Blind with rage, Xenia turned on the hot water full strength and the scalding water pouring out of the shower head splashed over Healy and the rest, sending everyone scrambling.

"Chief!" Felix Cruz reacted quickly, seeing his commanding officer go down, perhaps hurt badly. In a swift motion, he drew his taser from his jacket pocket and fired, hoping to subdue the suspect (with a dart carrying a high-powered electrical charge). Unfortunately the dart hit the bathwater before Xenia could scramble out and a staggering jolt of energy surged through the widow Dugan's body.

It was death by electrocution. The State of Ohio had always favored the electric chair. The good people of Palmer could now report, unfortunately, that the electric hot tub was just as effective.

CHAPTER 18

The postmortem on the Xenia Dugan affair was carried on in a number of venues. Jackie didn't take part in any of them, choosing instead to visit her mother's friend Maggie Mulcahy in the hospital. The older woman had a great many questions, which Jackie answered patiently.

"And what's to become of the wee children?"

"They've become wards of the city," Jackie responded. "There are a lot of couples looking to adopt good kids like the Dugan girls. I'm sure they'll find a good home."

"Their father doesn't want them?" Maggie asked incredulously.

"No." Jackie shook her head. "Big Bill Curtis still has dreams of making a political comeback. He's not going to do that with two illegitimate daughters who he fathered with a confessed murderer while she was still married to a Palmer policeman."

"That's a terrible thing," Maggie fussed.

"Oh." Jackie shrugged. "You can almost understand it. Her marriage with Matt Dugan was falling apart. She was a fairly attractive woman who wanted to have a full life, including children. Not an easy thing to have when your husband works most nights and has frequent bouts of alcohol-related impotency when he's home."

"Who told you this?" Maggie wondered.

"Marcella Jacobs dug it out," Jackie replied. "From Xenia's court-ordered psychiatrist. In a murder investigation the psychiatric records of the deceased become public record."

"Did she tell the shrink she committed all those murders?" Maggie asked.

"No," Jackie responded. "But she hinted at it strongly. Anyway, Xenia got pregnant and apparently tried to convince Matt that they were his twins."

"Which didn't work."

"Either that, or by that point Matt was just too far gone for even Xenia to stay with him." As Jackie talked she adjusted Maggie's special balsam-scented pillow so her mother's old friend could listen more comfortably. "Xenia moved out as soon as she was able and set up housekeeping in the apartment she had used with Big Bill Curtis. At first he agreed to help out with the upkeep."

"But that soon fell through," Maggie concluded. Like Frances, Maggie had worked for many years for the phone company and years of eavesdropping had taught her a few insights into the relationships between people.

"Yes," Jackie responded. "Big Bill was removed from office for accepting political contributions from gangsters. Then, with nothing to lose, he divorced his wife. As soon as their settlement papers became final, Xenia was stripped of her blackmail weapon and Big Bill cut her off without a dime."

"That really was too bad for her," the soft-hearted Maggie pointed out.

"No doubt about it," Jackie agreed. "So Xenia's only hope was Matt. But when she met with him to try to arrange a reconciliation, Xenia found out that he had been fired from the force. He was a disgrace. An alcoholic. No job. No prospects. The only assets Matt still had were his insurance and his pension. In order to get her hands on those, she not only needed Matt dead, she needed him dead fast, before he could jeopardize his benefits, or remarry or change his beneficiary to someone else."

"So she killed him?"

"Yes," Jackie answered simply. "And then she kept killing to hide her crimes. And then later, because she had killed so often, it became second nature to her."

"Very entertaining," Maggie said with a satisfied smile. "I'm glad you came by to tell it to me, Jackie."

Jackie held Maggie's soft, pink hand. "I'm just sorry I didn't get here sooner."

"Oh, a lot of people haven't come at all," Maggie said uncomplainingly. "You find out at the end, don't you, just what you've got and what you don't. Who's there for you and who moves away. It's a terrible thing to die, Jackie. I don't like it."

"I don't like it either, Maggie," Jackie said. She was on the verge of tears. "And because I don't like it, that's part of the reason why I'm always getting involved with chasing down murderers."

"Well, I want you to know, Jackie"—Maggie took a deep breath and then concluded—"that I think that what you do there at the university and whatever else you've done, like solving crimes, is just grand. You do good deeds. Don't let anyone tell you different."

"I won't, Maggie." Jackie smiled, winking down at Jake, who was looking up at her through the clear glass of the hospital room window. "I promise."

❖ CANINE CAPERS ❖

She's a film professor recovering from a failed marriage, but her real talent lies in detection. He's retired from the police force and has a nose for sniffing out crime–a wet nose. Together, Jackie Walsh and her crime-solving shepherd, Jake, make an unbeatable team.

By Melissa Cleary

__**DEAD AND BURIED**   0-425-14547-6/$4.99
__**A TAIL OF TWO MURDERS**   0-425-15809-8/$4.99
__**DOG COLLAR CRIME**   0-425-14857-2/$4.99
__**HOUNDED TO DEATH**   0-425-14324-4/$4.99

Holly Winter, the feisty, thirtysomething columnist for <u>Dog's Life</u>, has expertise in breeding, training...and collaring criminals. With the help of her big gray malamute, Rowdy, Holly keeps the unsolved mysteries in Cambridge, Massachusetts, on a tight leash.

By Susan Conant

__**A NEW LEASH ON DEATH**   0-425-14622-7/$4.99
__**DEAD AND DOGGONE**   0-425-14429-1/$4.99
__**A BITE OF DEATH**   0-425-14542-5/$4.99
__**PAWS BEFORE DYING**   0-425-14430-5/$4.99

Mysteries from the pages of <u>Ellery Queen's Mystery Magazine</u> and <u>Alfred Hitchcock's Mystery Magazine</u>. Includes tales from Margery Allingham, John Lutz, and Rex Stout.

__**CANINE CRIMES**   0-425-11484-4/$4.50

edited by Cynthia Manson